# THEY, ARE ALWAYS WATCHING

# They, Are Always Watching

## THINGS THAT GO BUMP IN THE NIGHT

Joseph Norris, III

writetoscare

# *Contents*

First Printing, 2022

## DEDICATION

To my late father, Joseph Norris, Jr.

# SIMONE

Marshall smiles widely looking above him at the marquee's bright golden lights. It reads, "Love, What Will You Discover?", starring Charlene Waters." His eyes harshly blink as the marquee lights suddenly go out. Still smiling, the brisk sharp cold wind pierces his fingertips. Conjuring thoughts of his dialysis needle sticks. Marshall cups his hands to his mouth blowing hot air into them.

"Can't believe I forgot my gloves."

He's outside of The Haynie Theater waiting for the star of the show, his wife, Charlene Waters. It's been a very long time since he's been able to venture out to see her perform. Two years ago, he was diagnosed with end-stage renal disease with his choices for dialysis treatments were doing it at home or at a dialysis center. At home, either Charlene or himself would do the needle sticks along with the connection to the dialyzer. Whereas at the dialysis center a nurse or a dialysis technician would do those procedures. Marshall chose the dialysis center; he was afraid to stick himself and Charlene's schedule didn't really permit her to do all that was encompassed. They both searched for an overnight dialysis center to enable Marshall to continue his freelance writing for the local newspaper in their hometown of Baltimore. Tonight, however, is a very special night. Very special indeed. There's a very new device that enables dialysis patients to dialyze while on the move. A portable, concealable, wearable, small, efficient dialyzer. Marshall jumped at the chance to get one and he's been using it for the last 2 months with no issues. Besides getting accustomed to sticking himself with a needle, no problem. When he wore it, every now and then he would pat his overcoat to ensure himself that it was still there because it's so light.

The metal swoosh of the side door of The Haynie Theater alerts Marshall of Charlene's coming.

"Great show tonight, Charlene. Have a wonderful evening." Terrence, the play's director said, holding the door open.

"Thanks, Terrence," Charlene said, pecking him on his cheek.

"Hi, Mr. Waters!!" Terrence yells.

"Hey Terrence, great show!"

"Thanks! Very glad you were able to come. Y'all be safe tonight."

As Terrence closes the metal door, Charlene rushes to Marshall. When they embrace she feels the dialyzer and pulls away quickly.

"Oh baby, I'm sorry," she said.

"Awww honey don't worry, it's indestructible, like me."

Marshall said, pulling Charlene close to him again.

"I am so happy you're here to view my performance," Charlene said, snuggling up under Marshall's arms.

They begin walking to their car, a few blocks away from the theater. The street has a few stragglers from the play and your normal horde of Saturday night partygoers. Contrarily, there is something else. Something else out there with them all. It's been watching Marshall since he left The Haynie Theater.

"Char, would you like to go to Mud's Eatery for a bite?"

"Sure would."

Marshall then looks at his watch, slowing down his walking pace.

"What's wrong?" Charlene asks.

"Oh, nothing. Still adjusting to the tightness of the catheter.

Don't worry, I'm good."

The tightness of the catheter from his body to the portable dialyzer was perfect, perfect at attracting macabre horrible attention. Reaching their car on the dank dark now empty street, Marshall opens the passenger door, pauses, embraces Charlene. Giving her a hard passionate kiss. Unexpectedly, Charlene's counter embrace becomes limp. Marshall, hearing a soft whimper, slowly rears back his face from Charlene.

Her eyes are glazed and very stoic. Her mouth is slightly ajar, when her head slides willingly to her left shoulder, dumping heavily to the cold asphalt ground. Marshall jerks away in abomination but his escape is stopped dramatically by their car. Her lifeless, blood-spewing body falls forward fully onto Marshall. Through the steam emitted from Charlene's severed nape, Marshall sees a woman standing directly behind her. The streetlights spawn shadows, hiding her face until she decides to step into the light. Butterscotch color skin, dark suffocating eyes encased upon a face exuding royal grandeur. Her long flowing thick gray dreadlocks sway slowly as she pushes herself up against the maimed body of Charlene, still being held by Marshall. This thing presses hard, then harder against them, forcing all three against the car, grinding. Marshall's eyes widened with horror are chained unmercifully by lust. Disgustingly, he begins to moan, blood flows rapidly to his penis and his dialyzer. His eyes close for a few seconds, feeling an orgasm coming. He should've kept them closed. That creature behind his wife has changed drastically. That butterscotch skin is now blackened, ashy and malformed. Her gaping mouth displays unsightly sharp jagged teeth. His last sight before those teeth are plunged deep into his chest, shredding skin of bone. She feasts heartedly, rapturously, and viciously.

When done, she releases both bodies who slam fast onto the bloody black street. That woman, that thing, is satisfied and sinfully regains her beautiful alluring facial form. In the distance, she hears laughter coming towards her area. Taking one last look at the despoilment she's inflicted, a smile encrusts upon her bloody lips as she leaps up to the dark rooftops for seclusion. Her body wears the darkness well, form-fitting, relaxing, foreboding and terrifying. Walking briskly along the rooftops, she slows down to stop, embracing herself, she feels the warm disrespectful blood percolating through her body. Abruptly, she hears blood-curdling screams coming from those who have discovered her lurid encounter. This brings a smile to her lorid face and energizes her for more.

Her name, Simone. One who thirsts for blood, one who knows what she is, a vampire, the undead. One that doesn't fear mortal trinkets like garlic, holy water or crucifixes, all mortal man's grandiose bull. Marshall was a novelty to Simone, someone completely intriguing and very different. His blood smells sweet and its taste was extremely delicious, clean, free of impurities and it aroused her, tenfold. Much different from any other blood consumed.

Renewing her trek along the gables of Baltimore, Simone has come to a new destination, an overnight dialysis center, with sweet-smelling blood. Marshall's blood has piqued her interest. Inhaling the stagnant cold air, she relaxes her body, crouching, as she waits to gorge again.

In her wait, she pulls a lavender kerchief from her bosom with the Gothic initials "LA" emblazoned on it. Smiling, she dabs the kerchief in a small puddle beneath her feet, wiping smeared blood from her face, hands and neck. With each touch of herself she moans while slowly sucking the blood from the kerchief.

"Hey mom! Wait right there! You're out early! Why didn't they call me!?" Van said, as he rushes to the dialysis center door to help his mother to the car.

"They did baby. I came out to see if your car was in the lot." Mrs. Meckley said.

"Mom, I didn't get a call. Here, slow down, let me help."

"I'm fine, baby. I'm not as tired tonight as those other nights. Just hungry. Maybe my body's getting used to dialysis. It's been what, 6 months?"

"No mom, been a year." Van said, holding open the door as his mother plops down in the passenger seat.

"Food might be hard to find tonight mom, it is 2:20 am." Van said, closing the car door, walking around the rear of the car, checking his cell for missed calls.

Two missed calls from the dialysis center are seen.

"Shit! I forgot to take phone off vibrate."

An immediate dull thud shreds the dead silent of the night. Van's car rocks down hard from a heavy force. Instinctively, he jumps away from his car's sudden violent movement when he sees on the roof of his car a sight no human can or should imagine. His mother, a waif of a woman, is being lifted out of the unopened sunroof by this thing. A grotesque entity of seemingly human flesh has embedded its right arm through his mother's head, lifting her higher. Then thrusting its ghastly foul mouth into Van's mother's stomach. Rushing to his mother's aid, Van vomits as he falls to the ground in anguish and terror.

"Stop, oh my God please stop." he gurgles, as he hears the violent manipulation of bones and flesh.

Instantaneously, Simone pulls her crimson laden face from Mrs. Meckley's body. Staring intently at the blubbering Van, then again she sucks deeply from his mother. Annoyingly, Simone's attention is drawn away again from her feast. Melissa, Mrs' Meckley's dialysis technician has come out for a smoke. She has yet to notice Simone, sobbing Van nor the ravaged Mrs. Meckley. It didn't matter. Simone makes quick work of Melissa by splitting her in half with her right hand nails. Blood, innards and a lone cigarette fountain down the dialysis center ramp. Snearing at Melissa's tainted blood, Simone returns to the fresh blood of Mrs. Meckley.

Getting her fill from her earlier partaking of Marshall and now Mrs. Meckley, Simone once again bounds to the rooftops. This time she's headed home, savoring the pure clean blood sloshing around inside her. The sun will be rising soon. Long ago she learned that the sun will burn her, killing her if there are not ample coverings covering her skin for protection. Tonight, unfortunately she's not prepared with ample coverings.

Her home, horror in plain sight to the public. It's an unwelcoming row home in Penn-North section of Baltimore. High impressive arched sublime red brick entrance with coal black double doors, floor to ceiling vertical windows clad in thick, maroon-colored drapes. The front entrance is precluded by an ominous porch and stairway, its faded greatness highlighted with lusterless red paint and snippets of white chipped marble steps. A six-foot wrought iron fence fastened by a paltry silver chain, locked with a gold padlock, secures the meager yard. Faint echoes of graffiti dinge some of the outer walls. Simone's adoration of this dwelling was at first sight back in 1919, the black oil street light post drew her. Its menacing flickering light signaled death to those that entered.

Now home, in her coffin within a coffin. Simone listens to the rats amble through the unholy unkempt hell hole. Dirt from her homeland of Burgaw, North Carolina is spread throughout. There is where she met the owner or that glorious handkerchief, Lord Almarth of Williamsport England in 1619.

He was a slave owner and a vampire with a strong love and attraction to fair-skinned slave, Simone. Many nights the pale, stout, damp-skinned, hollow-eyed Lord Almarth visited Simone. During one of their impromptu one-sided sex-capades, Simone was cut on side of her neck by one of his nails. Fighting the pain, Simone could not stop Lord Almarth from suckling upon her. Arousal of her yelps and moans intensified his sucking when he ceases.

"Tonight, I'm making you immortal, like me, my love."

Since then, Simone has been blood-lusting all over the world. Lord Almarth met his demise in 1837 in Chester County Pennsylvania to a Quaker with a quick sword. His beheading ended much grief and death in the area. Heartbroken Simone left the area.

Now she's in present-day Baltimore, Maryland, enticed by a new blood that intensifies and exhilarates her. She is not leaving.

That morning, the local news and Baltimore City Police along with some of the city of Baltimore are aghast, shocked, and downright scared shitless about the horrific events that occurred Saturday night. What kind of person would do this devastating horror movie autrocity and get away with it? The Police have video, tons of videos, but they only show the victims. Detectives Troy "KillerCowboy" Lewis and Diane "Watusay" Hurd are assigned to this case. Two tough veteran non-sensical flatfoots. Detective Lewis, gruff, wrinkled flannel shirt, dark blue jeans accented by black diamond-tipped cowboy boots. He used them, at times, to leave an unceremonious mark upon a perpetrator. Detective Hurd, fine-tuned, almost by the book, designer custom-fit pantsuit wearer. Her motto, "I ain't chasing nobody, that's what guns are for." They both weren't happy to be assigned this case, neither is fond of blood.

"This shit is crazy. Slicing off a woman's head. Pulling an old woman from the closed god-damned sunroof. Cutting a woman in half and draining two people of blood." Detective Lewis said, reading details of the case.

"Yeah. Four dead people. Two empty of blood and the other two dead but in a real fucked up way dead." Detective Hurd said.

"Hey people!! The killer or killers are not gonna turn themselves in you know!" Captain Jefferson yells.

"We're leaving, we're leaving."

Still daylight. Simone sleeps.

"How many dialysis centers are there in Northeast?" Detective Lewis asked.

"Let me see. Looks like five." Detective Hurd replies, looking at the small map in her hands.

"Seniority says you check out 3 and I'll take the other 2." Detective Lewis blurts.

"Fucking asshole." Detective Hurd mumbles.

"What did you say, detective!?"

"Nothing. And it's 'watusay'." Detective Hurd said, getting into the car.

"Yeah take the car, these two are walking distance anyway." Detective Lewis grumbles.

Canvassing the neighborhood and the 5 dialysis centers were useless. Not a soul saw anything except the aftermath of the carnage. Slightly dejected and a little cold, Detective Lewis stands on the corner as Detective Hurd pulls up.

"Nothing. Not a motherfucking thing. What about you?" Detective Lewis snarls.

"Zero for me too. It is Sunday, let's hit the dialysis centers again in the morning."

"Sounds good to me. All the centers gonna be watched by uniforms this evening anyway. Let's head home Detective 'watusay' Hurd."

Detective Hurd smiles. She got that nickname when she cussed at her supervisor, but he couldn't hear her and he kept repeating "What you say, what you say?" and it stuck.

Not a thing happens that night, nor the next few days or nights. No shootings, robberies, murders, nothing. Seems as though the criminals are afraid of what's out there. If they only knew.

The crisp tinge of Fall air greets Baltimore's anxious early risers. Terror from weeks ago has everyone still on edge. From the little evidence acquired and simple logic, Detectives Hurd and Lewis deduce that only the persons drained of blood were dialysis patients. A very weird macabre way to die. Both delved deep into the gang and occult groups for answers but they too were clueless, afraid and leary about what happened.

Alone in his townhouse eating a tuna fish sandwich, Rufus Chuck is preparing his arm for needle sticks. He's been training for the last month and a half for doing his own dialysis at home. The doctors and his family were very skeptical about Rufus doing this activity alone, especially due to his forgetfulness. Careful observation and training eased their minds.

Rufus is sticking to his own self-made schedule. Dialyze an hour from 8am to 9am, leave and run errands, hang out with the ole heads at the Hilltop Barber Shop, get takeout food for lunch, come back home to dialyze from 1230 pm to 2pm. Final dialysis will be from 8pm to 10pm, when his favorite tv programs are on.

His first session went smoothly, very little problem with the needle sticks. Some issues with the clean-up but very minor. After bandaging himself up, Rufus leaves home to go to the grocery store to play the lottery, pick up more tuna, some bread and apples; protein for his kidneys. After grocery shopping, to the Hilltop Barber Shop he goes to shoot the breeze with his friends Norton, Earnest, Kaiser and Sarge. Conversation was whimsical and manly degenerative with smidgens of respect to the women and children there to get cuts. There was very little chatter about those horrific murders a few weeks ago until Norton whispered to Kaiser.

"That crazy shit from last week still ain't solved."

Kaiser just shakes his head, then turns his head towards me.

"Rufus, how's that home dialysis thing going? You alright?"

"Just peachy keen and shit. I'm here talking with you mugs ain't I." Rufus siad, laughing.

Everyone laughs, even the women. Quickly the conversation switches to football.

"Almost forgot." Rufus said, reaching in his pants pocket, pulling out a medium size brown glass vial.

"What the hell is that, whiskey?" Sarge asked.

"No. It's liquid Vitamin D. I gotta take this too for my kidney health. I forgot to take some while I was being dialyzed this morning."

"Man, you 'spose to drink all of that each time?" Earnest asked.

"Yeah, but to be honest with you I haven't quite figured out how much. I'm still in training y'all plus I ain't never heard nobody die by od'ing on Vitamin D. Gotta go folk. Time to get my grub from Reeds then do my second session."

"Later!!" Everyone yells in unison.

At home, solemnly, Rufus sits in his recliner, rolls up his left shirt sleeve, wipes his pulsating fistula in his upper arm with alcohol wipes then sighs as he masterfully wraps the tourniquet. He takes one of the long 15-gauge needles from its sheath, then searches for a spot within the quivering large vein. The prick pain only lasts 10 seconds, but still, self-inflicted torture wasn't his cup of tea. Once that needle was in place, Rufus tapes it securely to his skin, connects the tube from the machine to the needle then proceeds to insert the other needle, following the previous procedure. Now that both needles and tubes are connected, he turns the dialyzer on, relaxes further in his recliner and turns on the tv. Local news is airing, and the reporter is doing on the street interviews with regular citizens on the devilish murders weeks ago.

"What are your thoughts on the grisly murders a few weeks ago?" the reporter asked a citizen.

"Man, them people was drained of blood. That's some vampire type stuff there."

"Vampire? True blood wasn't found in two of the victims but there is a rational explanation sir. Thank you." the reporter said, moving quickly away.

Rufus, shakes his head as he changes the channel to the vintage tv sitcoms channel. He picks up his corned beef sandwich next to two vials of Vitamin D and a glass of water.

"Remember to drink those vials when there's 45 minutes left on the machine Rufus." he said to himself, before taking a bite from the sandwich.

Those 90 minutes run by quickly, the dialyzer alarm indicating the session was over chimes loudly. Dutifully, Rufus closes the connection from the needles to the machine. Turns the machine off, pulls a needle from his arm while simultaneously placing a thick gauze upon the fistula to prevent blood runoff. Hard pressure is applied to the gauze until Rufus can replace his pressure with a tight plastic clamp secured with tape. The same process is done with the second needle. While both clamps secure the blood flow, Rufus rolls his eyes in disgust. He forgot to drink his two vials of Vitamin D. Begrudgingly, he opens each 50,000 IU vial, he's only required to take 1 vial, yet he swallows both down with his glass of water. Checking his fistula for bleeding, none is found. Rufus untapes the clamps, places a few extra strips of tape upon the fistula, yawning. This afternoon session has made Rufus a little weary. He goes to lay down to be ready for his 8pm session.

Concurrently, as Rufus sleeps, the unholy grumblings of hunger resonate deep within Simone. Soon she will be awake. Famished and ravenous for fresh, clean human blood.

Firecrackers and rockets sound off, echoing off of Rufus's ceiling. He exhales deeply, cracking open an eye while reaching for his alarm. That triumphant choice of sound effects for his alarm slightly bothers him. He feels more sleep is needed but his last dialysis session needs to be done.

Somewhere else in Baltimore, an eerie shift of cement sliding against cement indicates Simone is sliding her sarcophagus ajar. Her eyes, pure ivory white with tiny pinholes for pupils maneuver within her socket, seemingly haughtily estranged from her head. With adroit movements, she rises up out of the ¾ opening. As she steps out of her coffin, rats scurry to her feet. A wicked huff from her demon mouth sends them in a quick retreat. Meanwhile, Rufus has set up his dialyzer and is preparing to insert the first needle. That went well, the second needle not so. He missed the vein, blood speeds down his arm, under his elbow onto the pure white towel beneath. Quickly, Rufus grabs some gauze and alcohol wipes to clean up his mess. Simone too is creating a mess, she grabs a retreating rat, slicing its feral neck with her fingernail. Rich unclean rat blood cascades onto the squalid floor. Enraptured with the creature's demise, Simone watches its blood splatter as it squirms profusely in her cold elongated fingers. Her want for clean human blood pulls at her as she squeezes firmly against the rat's body, finishing it off and testing her will power. Tossing the remains of the rat against her dismal wall, Simone is joyful that she didn't sup. Rufus's joy came too, his from making contact with the second needle to get his blood flowing to the machine.

Simone begins her quest. Her direction is to one of the overnight dialysis centers in Charles Village. Upon getting there she witnesses several police cars a few blocks away. Not wanting distractions and useless entanglements, she lumbers along the rooftops to another dialysis center. However, there too are stationary police cars, waiting. Anger undertakes Simone along with her insatiable need to feed on fresh, clean human blood. Again, she decides no need for confrontation, so she scampers lightly across telephone pole wires, tree limbs and light poles to get to the next dialysis center.

Rufus's treatment is near complete. The two-hour session somehow rejuvenates his spirits and body.

"Oh no! Can't forget my liquid sunshine." Rufus said, picking up the two vials.

He had already injected 2000IU's of Vitamin D into the dialyzer and swallowed 4 1000IU each Vitamin D pill. He was making sure he got his full regimen or maybe even more of his daily supplement.

One mile away from Rufus's home, Simone's anticipation to feed abounds. She takes a brief stop to calculate her next move when she is captured by the smell of fresh clean blood with a stain of something different, something that flares her nostrils. Without hesitation, Simone dispatches to this new target.

Rufus cleans up his dialyzing area then sits in his body contoured seat preparing to chow down on an already prepared tuna fish sandwich. In a flash, as if the gates of hell were expelling a demon, Rufus's living room window explodes into his house. He tries his best to avoid glass and debris, yet he lay there fully covered in it. As he lays there on the floor bloodied, frightened and angry, he sees standing before him a figure of a woman. She stands above Rufus fully erect, surveying him. What light there is in his house is altered by confusion and dust, so details are hard to come by. Suddenly the woman speaks.

"There is something inherently different about your blood. It compels me imperiously."

"Fuck you bitc……."

His final words, Simone slices his throat with her index finger to swill gluttonously his life liquid. Rufus's blood pouches Simone's inner body with unrelenting vitality, lustfulness and strength. With Rufus fully drained, she releases him from her detestable grip. Rising to leave, she wants more, needs more. Taking a step towards the disintegrated window, Simone feels something she hasn't felt since her undead transformation eons ago, pain. A strong tightness squeezes within her belly and groin. This tightness begins to span throughout her cold body, forcing it to wilt over. Perplexed and angered by what's going, Simone stares at the sagging mound of flesh once called Rufus.

"What have you done to me!?"

Simone attempts to straighten herself up but this new affliction is too powerful. Her body tightens up more as blood, her blood, expunges itself from her eyes and other orifices associated with her being. Distressingly, Simone tries to move and get away from this new hell but her legs remain rooted. All at once, her skin commences to peel off her body in large chunks onto Rufus's floor. From these newfound body holes, small slivers of light are omitted. As seconds pass, the era of peeling evolves into sheer melting. Her body is melting from within. Rufus's overindulgence of his liquid sunshine is Simone's undoing.

# THE VAN

Half-awake as we speed down liberty road in Carroll County we're headed to a gig in Pennsylvania. Omar said this way was quicker but I think he's lost. I didn't care, the gig was tomorrow but we hadn't played in a minute so we needed to go through a walk-thru and sound checks. Cindy and Devin are stuck to one another, again, but at least they're asleep, no sex. Unexpectedly, the van swerves and our equipment scatter about the inside of the van. I lifted my head to tell Omar to slow down but he had already gotten the message. As I try to collect myself to settle down I look outside, stunned at how the moon cascades its eerie soft glow upon this dark desolate piece of earth. Up ahead in the distance on my side of the van, I see a figure walking towards us. Omar sees it too because he slows down more so for this figure is real close to the edge of the road. It's tall and slender wearing a red flannel shirt, black pants, and cowboy boots. It has a skull cap on over its waist-length stringy hair. Its head was lowered but the van's headlights show that its lips are moving, like it's talking. That drew my attention further down its body, trying to see if this is a dude or a babe.

"Oh my god!" I scream.

Omar jerks the van to the left away from the figure, Cindy and Devin release each other glaring at me.

"What the fuck is wrong with you!" Omar yells.

"That person, that thing, was carrying a human head!' I yell back.

By now Omar had stopped the van. We both look out the window to look behind us but see nothing, literally nothing. The bright moon left an inky blackness as if it too was frightened by that figure.

“You did see that, tell me you saw what that thing had in its hand!?" I stutter scream to Omar.

Omar looks at me then Cindy and Devin.

“I saw a person walking down the street, close to the road and I didn’t wanna hit him but I ain't see no head.”

'What!'

"Dammit hommies calm down, ya'll trippin n seeing shit, maybe it was a mirage." Devin said, pulling a joint from behind his ear.

Cindy reaches for the joint, but I smack it out of Devin’s hand which in turn leads to all four of us cussing and fussing. That all stops when we hear and feel something hit the rear outside of the van.

“What the hell was that!?" Omar screams, jumping out of the van.

Quickly I look in my side view mirror looking for Omar and that figure but see nothing. Devin takes a quick look too from the driver’s side window.

"Here he comes." Devin chuckles.

I move over to Devin to look in the driver's side mirror when the figure I saw walking down the street earlier appears in the window. It's a man. His face is yellowish orange with narrow eyes, long crooked nose and rotted teeth. Jumping back away from the window, I knock a screaming Devin and Cindy to the floor of the van. As we struggle to get up and try to keep our eyes on the widow and that man, we see it lift up his bloody left hand.

“This one fresh!” it roars.

Omar’s head dangles willingly from that man’s bloody clutches. Cindy, still screaming, jumps into the driver’s seat. With her eyes closed she somehow got the van in gear, and we speed off. Luckily we stayed on the road for the 15 or so seconds of her driving blindly and hysterically without hitting anything or ditching the van into the side of the road. She eventually opens her eyes allowing the flood of tears to pour out.

“What just happened!!? He killed Omar, he killed Omar, oh my god oh my god! He killed Omar!” Cindy screams.

"Calm down and slow down, I think we're far enough away from him now." I calmly said.

She slows the van down while looking in the rear-view window. Again, seeing nothing but blackness. She calls out to Devin. Getting no response, she sees he's passed out on top of our equipment.

"We've got to do something. Find a local cop. No, a state trooper. or maybe we should turn around and run that motherfucker over!' I snarl.

Cindy sits there with a deep empty look.

"Cindy, yo Cin..." I mutter, as I feel the van go in reverse then turn around.

"Cindy what ya doin?" I ask, in a childlike manner, trying to regain my balance.

No response, just her glassy eye stare out front window.

"Cindy what the hell are you doing!!" I scream, grabbing at the steering wheel only to be met by Cindy's teeth.

I quickly draw back to hold on tight to the dashboard. Cindy speeds the van up then abruptly slams the brakes. I hear a loud pop, indicating that a tire blew. We sit there surrounded by smoke and the darkness when I jump as a hand pulls on the seat from the back. Blood geysers up as an agonizing shriek makes me jump higher. Cindy has severed Devin's left hand.

"Oh shit, oh shit, what did you do, what did you do!? Dam dam dam!" I scream.

Devin has once again passed out. Cindy, still glassy-eyed and bloodied, looks at me scrunched down between the dashboard and the floor. She looks at the bloody knife in her hand.

"Did I get him?"

I didn't know what to say but 'yes'. Cindy's laying the huge knife on the middle console when the driver-side window explodes all over the both of us. As I duck my head to avoid the glass, from the corner of my left eye I see that man hoisting Cindy from the car with a meat hook engorged in her chest. Her crunching bones go in tandem with her screams. I then hear the words 'more fresh' then a loud thud. Suddenly no more screams, nothing. I stay prone to the position I'm in until I look up seeing how close I am to the passenger window. I scurry to the back of the van and pass Devin who's in bad shape. I grab some rags to wrap his arm when he whispers.

"Don't let me die tonight fuckface."

I smile and nod. Millions of thoughts are running through my head, what the hell is going on, two of my closest friends are dead, that man, that thing is still out there and I gotta save Devin and myself. Where the fuck did Cindy get that knife from? Have to clear my mind and think.

I look at all the shit in the back of the van. Rummaging around, really not sure what I am looking for, I grab two drumsticks, some guitar chords, duct tape and that last joint. Told Devin we'd fire it up when this is over. Looking at the stuff I've mustered up, I'm wondering how is this crap going to save us. I ask Devin if he's ok as I reach for Cindy's knife. Its weight feels good in my hand. Devin, seeing me admiring the knife, makes him uneasy. He holds his severed arm closer to his body.

"Dude this aint for you, no way man, this is for him," I said, tucking the knife under my shirt.

"It'll be daylight soon. I'm going to start this baby up flat tire and all and get us the hell outta here." I said, climbing to the driver's seat, trying my best to avoid Cindy's blood.

Turning on the engine and placing the van in drive, I look at Devin. He's smiling at my decision. His contentment quickly changes to fright. His eyes glow with fears. Quickly, my attention goes back to the road. Pure relief when I see what spooked Devin. A large moth stuck itself to the window.

"Only a moth Devin, I'll get it," I said, banging the window with my hand.

Three smacks of the glass and the beast releases itself. The van was moving pretty steady with three wheels. First house or town we see I'm stopping for help even though part of me wants to get back to Baltimore. I'm hoping I'm going the right way when smoke comes from the hood. The van rolls a few feet then stops.

"Not now. No no!!" I yell, banging my hand on the steering wheel.

Had to think, maybe the radiator needs water, but I didn't want to go out there. But I'm the only one. Devin's passed out, again. In going to the back of the van to get the water jug, my guess is, we've only driven 5 or so miles. Hopefully far enough from him. I walk back to the front of the van, slowly opening the driver door with a water jug and Cindy's knife in tow. As fast as I can, I jump out of the van and quickly pop open the hood. My dumb ass forgot to get a rag to open the radiator top. Yelling as I try to open the scalding top, I draw my hand back fast. Right into that thing's blood-soaked hand. I didn't hear, see or smell him. His grip buckles me. My wrist starts to crumble. My other hand has Cindy's knife. I jab it into his chest hard as I'm going down. It releases me. Gathering myself, I run to the back of the van, thinking I have to get another weapon. There's a shovel next to another water jug connected to the back door of the van that I've got to get open. Luckily it wasn't locked. I get it open when I feel a sharp hot sting in my upper back. I'm guessing it's Cindy's knife. Somehow, I manage to grab something as I spin around in pain. It was the water jug. I swung it viciously at him dousing him with what I now realize is gas, not water.

He grabs my flailing right arm and gets close enough to me that the details I saw from a distance were now blurry to me. His movement towards me pushes my back against the van and Cindy's knife deeper into me. Out the corner of my right eye I see a light. It's Devin. He has a drumstick with a wad of duct tape ablaze at the tip.

"Fresh meat this motherfucker!' Devin yells, throwing the blazing drumstick at him.

It hits him dead on as he burst into flames. Devin rushes to my side but I'm already very close to death. He hugs me tightly as he cries softly. He then reaches in his pocket, pulls out that joint from earlier and bravely walks over to our flaming attacker to light it up. As Devin stands there inhaling the joint, another pain jolts him. His burning flesh. Devin's face distorts agonizingly as he tries to get away but can't.

It now has a death grip on his ankle. Devin fights it, yet he too gets engulfed by the flames. Death swallows them all as the gurgling muffled words of the flaming entity ring out.

"Fresh meat........"

# RIDGE ROAD

Been a year since we've moved into this house, this neighborhood, this place. I still haven't met all my neighbors, don't really care. I'm more than content in going into our backyard and imagining I was somewhere else. Imagining I was somewhere else, I used to do that a lot in my bedroom. Now my sister Davita bugs me when I'm there so I took my act outside. She's not too fond of the outside, bugs, and stuff. At times my older brother, Lowry, would come in the backyard with me and we'd play but not too long. You see, I'm twelve and he's sixteen. That girl, Davita, is ten. This morning Lowry said he wanted to explore the backyard. Our parents always said stuff like, "our back yard is immense", "I love our acreage." All that meant nothing to me except, "big and pain in the butt to mow." I hate mowing grass. Luckily, Lowry and dad did all the mowing since we've been here. Guess they were letting me settle in. Well, I haven't.

"Lil dude, c'mon." Lowry said.

We're going to check out the stream we have, somewhere in the backyard. I grab the two walkie-talkies and run out of my room. Yeah my room, this house is a lot bigger than our old house. There I had to share a room with her. This house, we all have our own room, but she doesn't act like it.

'Where ya going?" Davita asked.

I tried to ignore her so I kept walking fast down the steps, not saying a word.

"Where the hell you going!!" Davita yells.

Stopping in my tracks and turning, looking at her..

"You better stop cussing or I'm telling ma!" I shoot back.

"Don't care. Where you going all fast and shit?"

Her cussing really bothered me a lot. Bothered ma a lot more than me or Lowry. Dad seemed bothered but he never said anything. The doctors said it was Davita's way of relieving the trauma and stress of losing our older sister Daniella to a boating accident two years ago.

"None of your business," I said, continuing on down the steps.

"Lil dude, let's go!" yells Lowry, from the deck that wraps around the house.

"Lil dude, let's go!" mocks Davita.

"I don't care where you go anyway, asshole." She said, walking back into her room.

I shook my head, thinking how pointless that little exchange was as I head to the sliding glass door.

"What you got there, Lil dude," Lowry said.

I stand there displaying the walkie-talkies in my hands.

"Our yard ain't that big," Lowry said.

Viewing the disappointment in my face, he snatches one of the walkie-talkies. As we were heading down the steps of the deck, we see the front door open through the sliding glass door. Mom and dad are home. They're carrying grocery bags.

"Boys, come help us with this stuff," Mom yells.

There goes our exploration. Lowry and I both exhale deeply and plod back up the deck steps and through the glass door. Mom was placing two bags on the kitchen counter and dad was walking in with three bags. Suddenly Davita comes running down the steps screaming.

"Grandpa Dickey, Grandpa Dickey!"

To mine and Lowry's surprise, it was our grandfather, Richard Sr., who we all called Grandpa Dickey. He was getting out of the car as the three of us ran to greet him.

"Hey my people, how y'all doin," Grandpa Dickey hollers, as he grabs and hugs the three of us.

Grandpa Dickey never called us kids or children; he always referred to us as 'his people'. We love Grandpa Dickey and we hadn't seen him in a long time. Matter of fact it was last year around this same time. I remember because he took the three of us trick or treating when we moved into this place. That was probably the best time I've had since we've lived here. Grandpa Dickey took us all to the streets and side spots in this neighborhood where we got tons of candy. Grandpa Dickey used to live in this neighborhood as a kid and he still knows people who live here, but he now lives in another state.

"Dammitt, why didn't you tell us you were coming!" Davita said, releasing her arms from grandpa Dickey's waist.

"Now, littlest person, we're gonna have to talk about your language." Grandpa Dickey said, smiling.

I saw mom motioning with her hands to get grandpa to not say anything about Davita's cussing but it was too late.

"Sorry, grandpa Dickey," Davita said.

Lowry and I looked at her in disbelief, she never apologized for anything. Grandpa smiles again and hugs Davita.

"Get some of these bags boys." Grandpa Dickey said, moving out of our way so we could get them.

"Littlest person, you carry this." Grandpa Dickey said, extending his hand to hers, indicating that he is her package.

That night at dinner, we ate and talked about all the fun we had at the old house and of course, mom and dad talked about the fun we can have here, at the new house. Then the conversation switched to Daniella. That conversation was short and brief; mom nipped it in the bud, quick.

"You kids know today is Monday, Halloween is Friday and Grandpa Dickey is here to take you all trick or treating. Your father and I have to leave to go to a conference Wednesday and we won't be back until Monday. This was met by cheers from me and Davita. Grandpa Dickey looks over at Lowry who's just sitting there with a blank look on his face.

"Don't worry, maybe you can stay home and greet the trick or treaters for me."

Lowry sat there thinking for a minute.

"Heck no! I'm coming with you guys. I want some candy too."

We ate our dessert and cleaned the table and helped mom wash the dishes. Dad and Grandpa Dickey went into the 'den' to talk and do I guess father/son stuff.

Later that week, Wednesday to be exact, we were taking mom and dad to the airport for their trip. We were riding down Ridge Road; I knew it was Ridge Road because all the houses on this road have little hills in their front yards or somewhere near the house. My dad said they were mounds used by ants to store food. There must be a ton of ants on Ridge Road. This is where Grandpa Dickey brought us last year for Halloween and we got all that great candy, but I don't remember these mounds. Grandpa Dickey's in the back seat nearly asleep, resting so he'll be awake when he drives back from the airport.

As we drive down the road I see Grandpa Dickey fidgeting in his sleep. Davita, Lowry and mom are fast asleep. I watch closely as Grandpa Dickey starts jerking his body and moving his arms like he is eating something. He really scares the crap out of me when he quickly opens his eyes very wide and inhales very deeply. Then he starts to mutter something. I jump away from him, bumping into Lowry, waking him up.

"We there already?" Lowry sleepily asks.

"No.... go back to sleep." I quickly said, not taking my eyes off of Grandpa Dickey. Who notices me staring deeply at him.

"What's the matter little one?" Grandpa Dickey asks.

"Nothing.....are you okay grandpa?"

"Sure am, what about you?"

"I'm good. I think."

Grandpa Dickey sits up, looks out the car window.

"Ridge Road, will be time soon." He mumbles.

"Time for what Grandpa Dickey?" A now awake Davita asks.

Grandpa Dickey smiles, hugging Davita.

"Almost time for a kiss, littlest person," he says, holding Davita in his arms.

I see dad look in the rearview mirror.

"We've got miles to go guys, let Grandpa rest. Dad, thanks for watching the kids for us."

"My pleasure son, my pleasure." Grandpa Dickey said, laying his head back against the headrest, still smiling this weird smile.

A few hours later we drop mom and dad off at the airport and we're headed back home. Funny, but the ride back home seemed quicker than the ride to the airport. We pull up to the house and I check the clock in the car, 4:37 pm.

"Lowry, take Michael and Davita into the house, make them sandwiches. I have to visit an old friend. Take care of my people and I'll be back in a few hours." Grandpa Dickey said.

Davita and I had already jumped out of the car and ran up the steps to the front door.

"Hurry up asshole, I'm hungry!" Davita yells.

"Littlest one, what did I tell you about your language!" Grandpa Dickey hollers, while handing Lowry the key to the house.

'Don't worry Grandpa Dickey, I'll take care of the brats. Please don't be too long though." Lowry said.

We all watch Grandpa Dickey pull off out of the driveway, then we go into the house. As time passes, we've eaten, played a few video games and begun watching a movie when there's a knock at the door. Lowry looks out the window by the door and sees Grandpa Dickey standing outside with three large boxes in his arms. Lowry quickly opens the door and takes the packages.

"Thanks. My people, these packages are for you."

"Grandpa Dickey brought us presents, Grandpa Dickey brought us presents." Davita sings as she unboxes her gift first.

"Wow! It's the bomb. I think." Davita said, pulling a long white dress with black strange lettering that wasn't English or any language I'd seen before.

"What's this shit!" She yells, holding the dress against her body.

"Littlest One! It's your costume for Halloween, a princess dress." Grandpa Dickey grimaces.

"Oh. Thanks, Grandpa Dickey."

"Go ahead, open yours too." Grandpa Dickey said.

I open mine next. It's a pair of long white pants with a long white pullover shirt with no buttons and the same funny lettering on it. I squelch up my face looking at the outfit when I see Lowry slowly opening his box. Same outfit thing as mine.

"Awww. C'mon my people, don't tell me you don't like them. These are the outfits worn by kings and queens back in the olden days when they went out on Halloween for a special event." Grandpa Dickey, said excitedly.

"Ok, kings and queens dressed up in this for candy?" Lowry asks.

"No, not candy. At this special event you all get money. Loads of money. I thought we'd do something very different and special this year for Halloween." Grandpa Dickey said, with a huge smile taking over his face.

"Money. Loads of money. I'm in. But do we have to wear this outfit?" Lowry quips.

"Yes. That adds to the specialness of this Halloween event. You all will not look like any of the other kids. The more unique your costume the more money you get."

I'm still standing there, holding my costume, with a smirk on my face.

"How come we didn't do this last year Grandpa Dickey?"

"You see, this is the 500$^{th}$ anniversary of the 'money' for Halloween event and I got you three to be the guest of honor. That's what my meeting was about earlier."

"Guest of honor. Damn I'm good!" Davita yells.

"Go get some sleep now, tomorrow we'll go to the movies and see whatever y'all want to see."

This is met with great cheers from the three of us!!

"A movie within reason, we all have to be able to view it." Grandpa Dickey hollers, over our cheers which ends in jeers.

Just then, the phone rings. Davita runs over to answer it with the outfit still in her arms.

"Hello."

"Hi sweetie. This is daddy. Let me speak to Grandpa Dickey."

"Okie fuc..."

"Davita!!" Dad screams over the phone.

She slowly removes the receiver from her face, handing it to Grandpa Dickey.

I hear dad say that they arrived safely. They talk briefly then Grandpa Dickey makes us go to our rooms for bed. I'm kind of excited about getting money and candy for Halloween, never got money before.

The next day is spent in the movie theater. Viewing a kiddie movie for Davita then Grandpa Dickey relented and we all watched a scary movie later that day. I was still pumped and excited about tomorrow. The movies wore us out and we all went straight to sleep once we got home.

The next morning was a typical Friday morning with Grandpa Dickey, something that we all loved. Scrambled eggs, bacon, sausages, waffles, grits and cranberry juice for breakfast. We all ate till we were so full we all wanted to go back to sleep. As the day passes we watch the cut-down versions of horror movies on TV and hand out candy to the trick or treaters. It's getting dark when Grandpa Dickey comes downstairs dressed in a costume, surprising us because he didn't tell us he was dressing up too. His costume was strange and weird, scuba diver gear but without the tank.

"What? Oh my costume. I'm a deep-sea diver. I've got to dress up for the special event too." Grandpa Dickey said, with that big strange smile on his face.

"Why your shit don't look like our shit?" Davita asked.

"Littlest one. Your mouth will be the death of me. My people, go get dressed. We have to make several stops before 11 pm, that's when all the fun begins. My costume is different because I'm not getting any money. Remember you three are the guests of honor." Grandpa Dickey said, rushing us up the stairs to get ready.

We rush upstairs to put on our costumes. In a few minutes, the three of us come downstairs, high eyebrowing each other as we gander at each one in their outfits.

"My people. You all look perfect and money worthy." Grandpa Dickey said.

"Cool. Let's go collect." Lowry said.

"Before we go, here, take these." Grandpa Dickey said, handing the three of us large trash bags.

We stare at him and the trash bags.

"Gotta carry your stash in something." Grandpa Dickey said.

Relieved, I thought he was putting us on leaf duty or something.

We venture out. We've collected tons of candy but no money.

"I ain't got no cash Grandpa Dickey. What's up with that!?" Lowry screams.

"You'll get what's due to you on Ridge Road. Be patient." Grandpa Dickey said, still smiling that weird smile.

It was near 11 pm, my walkie-talkie, which I bought, just in case, read 10:46. I look ahead and see that we are headed to Ridge Road, but there are no lights on any of the houses. It's pitch black. I tug Lowry by his arm. Davita is walking with Grandpa Dickey.

"Lowry. I don't think Ridge Road is doing Halloween. Nobody has their lights on and where are the other kids."

Lowry looks around and notices the darkness too. Up ahead Davita and Grandpa Dickey are still walking. They're on the first block of Ridge Road.

"Grandpa Dickey, ain't' no houses lights on. They ain't doing Halloween!" Lowry yells.

"Yes, they are!" Grandpa Dickey, screams back.

Suddenly we see the flickering of lights outside on the street. Lowry and I slow our walk down Ridge Road when we both see figures walking around those dim flickering lights. We walk a little further when we see this man walk up to Grandpa Dickey and Davita. He's dressed in a scuba outfit too, carrying a big box which he opens showing the contents to Grandpa Dickey. Davita shrieks and jumps up and down frantically, Lowry runs to her. I'm too afraid to move.

"Money! Motherfuckers! Money!" Davita screams.

Now I run but stop when I notice we are surrounded by other people dressed in scuba outfits. I also observe there are more lights on around those mounds. As I look closer, I see the mounds are actually moving. I try to corral Lowry again but can't, too many people around us. I begin yelling for Grandpa Dickey but that yell goes to a whimper. That man in front of Grandpa Dickey and Davita leans down and takes a bite out of the side of Davita's little head. That's when the others start attacking and eating us. As teeth and nails dig into me and Lowry, my last vision is of Grandpa Dickey, joining in on the feast of Davita. Biting off her lips.

# OUT HOUSE

"It's just sitting there boy." That's what Joe, my pa, used to say.

I haven't been to it, the outhouse since he went there and never came back. I was ten when that happened. I'm 16 now and we have indoor plumbing. Been many a day and night I sit in my room watching out my window, waiting. My ma, Hattie-Mae, and other kin swear I'm pining away for Joe to come back. I keep telling them he can't come back but they ain't studying me.

Saturday morning, Hattie-May sees me sitting on the porch whitlin' a duck call. I was whitlin' away, not paying attention to the wood in my hand but staring at it, the outhouse. Without cause, Hattie-Mae starts screaming and fussing something fierce. My attention goes straight to her then I feel it. Uncivilized pain shoots through my fingers, hands, and arm. My dumb ass done whittled clean to my bone. Blood had already pooled all up on the porch. I jump up like a scared jackrabbit from the porch and go screaming and crying right into the woods. In my craziness, I look back at Hattie-Mae to see if she was following me but she wasn't. She was down on bended knee, spitting fiercely on the porch as she wipes up my pool of blood. I hear her yell my name along with God, Jesus, Mary and any other saintly person she could muster. Not too sure why I ran, especially not into the woods anyway. But it led me right into Jeb. Probably there, hunting, fishing or shining.

"Hey there Blue, where's the ho-down you rushing to?" Jeb said, as I zip by him near the catnip grove, tripping over a vine.

Jeb quickly grabs my overall straps, lifts me and stops me from falling onto the ground. He sees me crying then he sees my blood.

"Well damn Blue. What the hell you done did now?"

I clutch my hand closer to my chest when Jeb quickly pulls it away. He's a big ass strong country boy, that Jeb. Big, 6 feet 5 big, husky, solid, big-boned. His strength comes from toting bales of tobacco five miles away to Rudy's Ridge so they could weigh it, divy it up then ship it off to Walnut, Mississippi. Jeb's totes were at least 150 pounds, that's what he told me anyway. I trust and like Jeb, even though I hate that he calls me Blue. Just 'cause I got a hand size birthmark on my left cheek that's bluish, ain't no reason to call a boy something he ain't.

As fast as Jeb toted me in the air he was even faster at placing my ass up on a huge rock. He pulled a huge hunk of wood from his back pocket.

"Bite this! You don't want the ground tasting your blood." Jeb said, while patting my wound and shirt with herbs and bark he got from the ground.

I'm young, but I thought what Jeb said was dumb and was doing even dumber. The herbs and bark came from the ground that he said didn't need to taste my blood. That thought lasted a second. The herbs burn my skin making me bite down hard and unruly on that hunk of wood in my mouth.

"There. You should be squared away now Blue. I don't wanna know how you did that nor rightly care. Jus' know you better take your narrow ass back home and keep this tied 'round your hand. The bleeding has stopped but jus' in case. Now git." Jeb said, handing me a black bandanna to wrap around my wound.

I still feel bad about that day 'cause I never said "thank you" to Jeb. I do remember turning around to say something to him but stopped 'cause I saw him burning the herbs and tree bark he used on me in a tin can. That was very crazy and weird to me. I just hurried on home. When I got there, Hattie-Mae was asleep at the dinner table, probably waiting for me. I go straight to my room and unwrap the bandanna. It doen't hurt and the wound is closing up. I look at it for a minute then go to my usual spot. My window, to stare at it. The outhouse.

The next morning had me still awake, staring out the window. My bedroom door squeaks open.

"You're back. I reckon your hand is ok." Hattie-Mae said.

I didn't answer her.

Angry, she grabs me by my shoulder. "Boy, your Joe ain't never coming back. He ran off with some town floozy, leaving me here with you!"

Hattie-Mae releases me, pauses, then walks out slamming my door. I resume my waiting.

The afternoon is flickering away. Thoughts of all the times others went to the outhouse and came back ran through my head. Why am I so spooked by it and why did it take Joe. I saw what happened that night. I was woken up by Joe knocking over a bucket used to feed the chickens. I saw him with a lantern walking to the outhouse. It was a spooky creepy night. The tree's limb shadows looked like an army of grim reapers trying to get a piece of him. Pa zigged and zagged through their clutches. I watched him open the outhouse door when he quickly looked at his hand. Not sure why he did that. He then hung the lantern on the nail above the shit pail before closing the door. A few minutes later a ghostly mist started rising up around the outhouse. At first I thought it might be that thing called methane. I heard of methane gas but I ain't never seen it. It got thicker and thicker then the outhouse started shaking.

"Son of a bitch!" pa yelled.

Then just like it came, it was gone, the mist was no more. The lantern light was gone too. I ran to Hattie-May's room, waking her. She was in a corn liquor stupor. Leaving her, I ran back to my room, looking out my window seeing only the faint shadow of the outhouse in the dim moonlight, no Joe. I was way too afraid to go out there and check on him. I just crawled under my bed, crying and cursing.

The next day.

"Hey Blue. Boy, you hear me? Your hand feelin ok!?" Jeb yells.

He's outside my window. I smile, showing him my hand with no wrapping. He smiles back, gives me a thumbs up, and starts walking to the outhouse. My eyes jump with fright.

"No Jeb. Don't go in there!" I yell, opening the window.

He kept walking but I know he heard me 'cause he raised his hand. I guess he has to do what he has to do. It's still daylight so maybe nothing will happen. Minutes pass, Jeb walks up to the outhouse then goes right past it into the woods. Some relief for me but he riled me so much I didn't think to ask him what he meant by saying 'don't let the ground taste your blood' and why he burned the herbs and bark.

Nothing left for me to do but my chores and my watch. I head to the front room to get ready to feed the chickens, mend the pigpen and go to the General Store for some flour and sugar. Hattie-Mae is at the stove frying up some bacon. When I walk in she never turns my way.

"Boy, here's the money for the sugar and flour. I done already fed the chickens. When you get back mend the pig pen!"

"Fine."

I take her money that she gets for cleaning Miss Forbes house 3 days a week. Walking towards the back door I turn to Hattie-Mae.

"Yesterday Jeb said, 'don't let the ground taste your blood'. What's that mean ma?"

Hattie-Mae, still not turning to face me.

"Jeb was probably liquored up. Plus, he talks stupid and dumb. Go get my shit boy, now."

That made me madder than a hornet with no damned nest to return to so I leave the house in a rush. Before I got too far, I turn, staring at the outhouse. There's a breeze blowing leaves and dirt around our property, but the breeze seems to avoid the area around the outhouse. My looking stops when I hear the screen door on my porch crack the backside of the house. Hattie-Mae's came outside. To avoid a whoopin, I ran towards the General Store.

After a mile or so of running, I slow down, noticing how peaceful and noisy it is at the same time. I felt safe, welcomed by the woods. The animals and insects seem like they are talking to each other. I love living in the woods. Everything but that outhouse. Why do we still have that thing anyway? We don't use it anymore. Only Jeb, a few townies and hunters passing through use it but they all leave it.

"Howdy Blue."

"Howdy Parson Wright."

I'm now on the outskirts of town and coming up on the General Store quick fast and in a hurry. On the rickety worn wooden porch of the General Store sits Mr. Slice, pa's old hunting buddy and Ole Man Zock. They were jib jabbing away at each other until I walk up on the porch.

"Hey Blue, oh I mean Sonny, how's ya ma?" Mr. Slice asks.

"She's fine sir. Doing fine."

Ole Man Zock just gawks at me through those magnifying thick glasses he wears. At least I think he was gawking at me.

"Your hand boy. You cut it?" Ole Man Zock asks, his face pointing to the black bandanna wrapped around my hand. Even though the wound is closed, the bandanna made me feel good.

"Yes sir….."

"Cut it where?" Ole Man Zock asks, cutting me off.

"....huh? My hand. See, I cut my hand."

"No boy! Were you in or out of the house?" Ole Man Zock asks, very slowly.

"I was outside."

Both men slowly sit back in their ragged worn adirondack chairs.

"Outside. Outside where, boy?" Mr Slice asks.

"On the porch, then I ran into the woods but Jeb grabbed me, stuck a piece of wood in my mouth, threw me on a big ass rock then put herbs and tree bark on my wound real fast."

"That Jeb. Good boy. Real good boy that Jeb." Mr. Slice said.

"Glad you're still here boy." Ole Man Zock said.

"Yeah. Thank y'all." I said, rushing by them to get into the General Store. Not sure what they meant by 'glad you're still here boy'.

After a few minutes inside, I get Hattie-Mae's stuff and pay for it. I'm kinda hesitant in going back outside and dealing with the two ole cogers on the porch but I go. They were going at it again, gabbing at the mouth. This time they were talking 'bout Dewey Flagg. They stop when I come fully out.

"Get on home boy. Keep that cloth tight. Remember, no blood drippin." Mr. Slice garbles.

Once outside of town I start thinking more about Dewey and the woods. The old wives tale say a little after the Civil War, these slaves, 100 or so, men, women and children were killed. They were thrown into a huge hole. No coffins, no prayer no nothin. One of the slave women was Mamma Ruby. A tall, big, beautiful, strong Black woman. Many say she had the skin that looked like creamy chocolate cake. She also had powerful words of wisdom and the most ornery slave healer folk in Kyoca County. They say before they killed her, she spouted out words to them white folk.

"Our blood mixed with this here earth will be cursed. Those that blood feeds the ground after we dead will be taken."

Some years later, Dewey and some boys were leap froggin by Peoples Creek when Dewey jumped over a boy and slipped. His face hit the ground, breaking his nose. Blood runs down his face, splattering on the ground. Slowly this strange fog comes out of nowhere surrounding Dewey and the other boys. Folk say the boys halled ass out of there, all but Dewey. The mist or whatever, held Dewey tight. According to Denny Caraway, who looked back at Dewey, he saw one by one, Black mangled hands holding Dewey from his legs to top of his head. They say they heard a faint scream from Dewey but it was muffled by an eerie pop. Dewey's body exploded, blood shot everywhere all over the woods. Denny said just as fast as the fog came it was gone. So were the mangled hands, the mangled arms and Dewey.

With all that thinking about Dewey and our county's crazy legend I didn't realize I'm in front of my house until I hear Hattie-Mae.

"Took you long enough. Somethings wrong with our toilet. Plumber said septic tank or some newfangled shit hole thang. We gotta use the outhouse till we get inside toilet fixed." she said, taking the stuff from my hands.

"I ain't going up to that thing!" I yell.

With her free hand, Hattie-Mae slaps me. I fell backwards onto the ground, well aware to protect my left hand in the fall.

"Boy! I told you 'bout sassing me!"

As I lay there, the path to the outhouse comes into view. During the day that path is scary as hell. At night it's a tutoring nightmare. You have to walk past the chicken house. You hear them scratching the ground and that funny chicken sound they make but you can't see them. The same for the pig pen. It's across the path from the chicken house. At night you hear their crazy demon grunts and squeals then them floating dull bloodshot eyes.

"Get up boy! Clean yourself up. Mr. Middleton is coming to visit!"

Not happy to hear that, but I trudge myself up to go to the bathroom. The water in the sink still works so I start washing dirt off myself. When done I'm putting on a clean shirt when I hear Hattie-Mae greeting Mr. Middleton at the front door. Them two start caterwauling and laughing immediately. They were old friends, way before she met Joe. Me and pa didn't care much for their friendship. Even so, out of respect for my elders, I leave my room to greet Mr. Middleton.

"Well, lookit here. Blue. How you is boy?" Mr. Middleton said.

"I'm ok."

"You done grown a lot since last time boy. Hope you taking care of ya momma boy."

"Yes. I am."

"Butch. Come on over here. Let Blue be."

Mr. Middleton gives me this weird wide smile, slaps me on my shoulder and heads over to Hattie-Mae sitting at the table. The table is set with a bottle of shine, cornbread, catfish and string beans. I was offered food but I ain't want none. I go back in my room to lay down. As I lay there, thoughts of my day at the general store run through my head.

That's interrupted by Hattie-Mae.

"Butch! You stop saying stuff like that!"

"Hattie-Mae you know it true!"

"Stop! Blue might hear."

"I was by the General Store when I see Blue leaving. Mr. Slice and Ole Man Zock were on the porch talking about Dewey and the slave hole." Mr. Middleton said, lowering his voice.

"Stop it now Butch."

"Fine. I gotta whiz anyway."

"You gotta use the outhouse, our indoor toilet ain't working."

"Really? Out there in the dark?"

"Here's a flashlight, chicken."

Quickly I get up from my bed and rush to my window. In minutes I see the dim beam from the flashlight cut slowly through the dark. Mr. Middleton finds the path to the outhouse. He shuffles up the path, I guess trying not to rile the chickens. He did scare the pigs though. Their squealing and grunting scared him too, his dull flashlight flounders all over the place. Once he got himself together, he made it to the outhouse. I see him enter, then close the door. I don't know why but I'm sweating like a pig and breathing funny. I'm looking for the mist but I ain't see none, even after minutes go by. Then I see that dull flare of a flashlight coming from outta the outhouse. Nothing happened. Mr. Middleton got closer to the house and I hear Hattie-Mae on the porch.

"Hurry up Butch. I gotta go too!" she yells, in her corn liquor state.

"Yeah, yeah woman. Hold on, here I come."

I see the pale light being exchanged. Hattie-Mae angrily ambles up the path, grumbling, upsetting the chickens and the pigs.

"Hattie, Hattie-Mae! Be careful up there. It's a bunch of nails punched the wrong way on the door. Some fool got the points backwards!"

"I know dammit! Put them there myself!"

Did I hear her right!? She put nails with the points sticking through the door. Why!? I continue watching her make her way. Once there she opens the door, and the failing flashlight goes out.

"Shit! Shit! Shit!" Hattie-Mae yells, banging the flashlight against the door.

It comes back on, followed by a blood-curdling howl.

"Nooooooooo!"

Straightaway, a mist encloses the outhouse. The chickens and pigs silence themselves. A loud muffled pop is heard then the mist slowly goes away. Hattie-Mae does not exit the outhouse. My guess is, she's where Joe is, along with any slave owner or persons whose blood, is tasted by the woods.

# MR. BITTERS

Twenty-four days, eleven hours and thirty-seven minutes, Jason has been home from the hospital from kidney transplant surgery. He was to have a home care nurse visit three times a week, but he lied and told the doctors that his live-in girlfriend Melissa is a nurse. Truthfully Melissa is his ex. Two months ago, they were a loving, viable couple. Jason was an investigative reporter and Melissa was owner of a fashion boutique in Washington DC. Before Jason's operation, he and Melissa argued a lot, over anything and everything. One fight was over Jason's investigation of the Carlito crime family and how she wanted him to stop and leave it alone. But the big fights were over Melissa's disapproval of his extended family not trying or even asking to be tested to see if they'd be a kidney match. That argument led to things being thrown and harsh hurtful words, making Melissa leave the house.

The day Melissa left the house, Jason's lone neighbor, Mr. Bitters, was a witness. He was doing his daily normal routine. Slouched heavily in his tattered, worn, duct-taped lawn chair. Drinking from the rested elephant mug on his bulbous belly. On the weary porch is a medium-sized bottle of whiskey along with a pristine white paper cup filled with lemon wedges. Mr. Bitters never looks in the direction of the arguing couple. Not even after Melissa slammed the front door and ran down the walkway screaming then driving off. Mr. Bitters' eyes stay focused on an area across the street from both houses. A gully, a deep green reserve of brush, dying trees, uncut grass and trash. Shit discarded by passersby in cars or on foot.

"What up Mr. Bitters," Jason said.

Mr. Bitters nods his head slowly, sucking nonchalantly on a lemon slice. He never turns to Jason. Still focused on the gully. Jason shakes his head while looking in the direction Melissa's car sped off to.

"Shit! Those lazy, no-good motherfuckers!" Jason yells, noticing something in the gully.

Mr. Bitters never said a word. Sucking on that lemon slice, still staring at the gully.

"That big ass trash bag has been there since before I left for my operation. I've called, sent pictures and emails but it's still there!" Jason yells.

Suddenly Mr. Bitters turns his head to Jason. He squints his eyes, snorts his nose, pours more whiskey in his elephant mug then spits in Jason's direction.

"What the fuck!" Jason screams, quickly moving out of the way of Mr. Bitters' lugee.

Gearing up to spit back, he changes his mind.

"Crazy old fucker." Jason mumbles, going back inside his house.

A tan alley cat slinks towards the trash bag in the gully. It stops about 5 feet from it, arches its back then hisses loudly. Mr. Bitters leans forward to see clearer when the cat howls loudly and makes a quick retreat, bounding in the opposite direction of the trash bag. Jason seeing this interaction just shrugs his shoulders while continuing on into his house. He goes directly to his pc, checking for emails from Melissa. Only emails seen are junk emails, some emails from the hospital, and one from The Nelky Cruise Funeral Home. Immediately he marks them all as "Spam" then deletes them. Pain in Jason's knees and elbows begins to set in. As he limps to the kitchen to get his meds, a deep burning and extreme soreness erupts in those earlier places. His meds are on the table in the kitchen, the table Melissa brought from Jason's ex-neighbor Rachel, another argument. His meds are pretty potent painkillers that work very fast. He only took two because he didn't want to overdo it and pass out, plus he wants to get back into his writing. The clock on the oven reads 4:15 pm.

"Shit. It's late. Fucking with Mr. Bitters and Melissa, too much."

Jason sits down at his pc when he hears a loud heavy vehicle barreling down his street.

Getting up as best and fast as he can, he makes it to his door to see what's making the noise.

"Bout motherfucking time!"

Coming down the street is a city trash truck. Jason watches it scuttle down his street without stopping.

"Hey!! Hey!! You're supposed to stop assholes! Pick up that damned trash bag! Hey!" Jason screams, slinging his door open, wrenching in pain as he waves his arms to get the trash truck driver's attention.

Slowly, Jason pulls his cell phone out of his pocket. His wrists and elbows are now burning more so. The city's sanitation department is on speed dial. Writhing in pain, he does his best to be patient as the phone rings and rings. He turns to Mr. Bitters' porch to see the old grouch had gone inside. The sanitation department's phone picks up but it's the answering machine.

"Shit!"

Jason listens to their spiel then leaves a message.

"Look! This is Jason Komorebi at 4937 Dunkirk Ave. One of your trash trucks just came down my street and did not stop to pick up that large trash bag that I've been calling, emailing, and leaving voice messages about. If y'all won't get rid of it then I will!"

Frustrated, Jason goes back into his house to take one more painkiller pill. On top of the refrigerator, he sees a book of matches. For some weird reason, his pain has subsided, and he doesn't take that extra painkiller. Instead, he takes those matches and trudges back to his front door. Making it down his steps, Jason decides to set that trash bag on fire. Any consequences he can blame on teenagers of Mr. "Crazy Ass" Bitters.

As he gets closer to the trash bag in the gully, the pain comes back intensely. All of his joints are aching and burning. Stumbling forward hard, Jason lands right on top of the trash bag. The initial feel of whatever is in the trash bag startles him. His attempts to push himself off of it fail as he continually falls onto the trash bag. Angry now, Jason rolls off of the trash bag to set himself free. Right now, his whole body is on fire with pain. His inquisitive burning desire to now see what's in this trash bag is trumping his pain. Writhing in pain on the ground, Jason manages to scoot himself up to the tightly tied opening of the trash bag. It's tied with three twist ties and two strands of rawhide. In his weakened painful state, he cannot untie any of the wrappings. Pissed but not conquered, Jason remembers his book of matches in his shirt pocket. Gingerly pulling them out, he makes several failed attempts to light them. With one more painstaking gut-wrenching effort, he's able to light one. Carefully he burns the rawhide twine then the plastic twist ties. Slowly, he widens the bag to view its contents.

Aghast with shock, Jason rears away from the trash bag, his mouth is agape, his eyes sear with terror as morbid contents tumble out. Severed limbs and a head. A very recognizable head. His head. The words "dead writer" are carved into his forehead. On Mr. Bitters porch, members of the Carlito crime family greet and hug him. They're laughing, pointing at Jason's house then to the trash bag, in the gully.

# TOWN

Hard time sleeping last night. Kept hearing those voices telling me how great this town is and how everyone loves me. I enjoy where I'm living now, but don't love it. The neighbors were ok I guess, except maybe one, but he can be dealt with.

A lot has changed here since my moving in 6 months ago. My life seems to be at ease, with very little worries. Help was all around, people became nicer and crime, all around the town literally came to a standstill. I knew I had nothing remotely to do with all of this but according to Ms. Barbara up the street, I was the reason. If that's the case, then maybe I need to move to different spots in Baltimore to end crime. What a joke. You see, it was this that also kept me awake. I knew I had to leave and move out of this town. My company knows I'm a good problem solver and the problem they had in downtown Baltimore was resolved. The house in this town, Acer Hill, was the closest they could find near downtown Baltimore that wasn't crazy expensive. Next gig I have is in Ohio.

Years ago, my family moved out of this little enclave of a town. An elder, Mr. P. Pye told me it was a really cold day in hell when my family moved. Wasn't sure what he meant by that, but he and the town council were ecstatic that a Middleort was moving back in. This morning I decided to roll out without saying a word to anyone, especially the town council and Ms. Barbara. I didn't pack much when I moved in so this should be easy peasy. What I have in the house fits in my trunk and back seat. It was just me anyway; plus, my job had already okayed the move. All I had to do was roll out.

Opening my door, exhaling, there is a sort of relief as I head for my car. The veiny blue sky, sullen with swollen clouds, slowly clogging the arteries of sunlight, presents itself as mean and menacing to me. I'm not a morning person so any sky would probably look that way to me. Opening my car door, I feel eyes piercing the back of my head. Turning around, I see him. Charles. He waves and is saying something, but I couldn't stand that motherfucker, so I quickly wave as I jump in the car. "It's way too early in the morning for his shit." I thought as I started the car and pulled off. I had gotten a block away from the house when I heard something hit the rear of the car. My first thought was that punk-ass Charles threw something at my car but he's no longer outside when I stop and jump out of the car. Looking around, I see no one. Pissed, I walk to the back of my car and see a big blackbird on the ground. Its feathers were ruffled and blood oozes out of its eyes. My trunk had a big ass dent in it.

"Dammit, Dammit!!!" I yell, kicking the bird halfway across the street, still looking for Charles or anyone for that matter.

Walking back to the front of my car I notice dozens of big black birds in the bare tree in Mr. Davis's yard. They are silent, looking in my direction, not moving. I hesitate a little while looking at them, then quickly open my car door when I feel a sharp crushing blow to the back of my head. A big ass blackbird was dive-bombing me and it was coming back. Frantically I swat at it but it keeps coming. Out of the corner of my eye in my fight with the big ass bird, I see the other birds still on the branches, motionless. I manage to get my door all the way open, leaping into my car. The window is up so it couldn't get in, but it sure as hell tried. The engine is still running so I put it in gear and sped down towards Hannibal St Bridge when I see the other birds are now moving. These fucks begin attacking my car to get to me. Dammit, it's too many of them. I can't see, my driving is out of control so I slow down the car and start blowing my car horn repeatedly. This disperses them a bit. Giving me a chance to turn the car around and head back to my old house. Weird, but as I get closer to the house, the attacks die down yet I can barely see. My windshield is cracked and bloody with dead birds beaks embedded in my windshield. My side windows and rear window are fucked up too. In an instant, like magic, the birds were gone, nowhere in sight. Slowing down to a stop, I get halfway out of my car, getting a good view of dead birds all over my car, feathers, claws, beaks, blood, brains, and shit.

In my front yard, I see Charles, Ms. Barbara, Mr. P. Pye, and all the members of the town council.

"Did ya'll see what just happened! Why the fuck are you all on my property!!!?"

They just stand there, smiling.

"Mmmmm.... Is this still yours!? Thought you were leaving!?" Charles barks.

"Looks like you have car trouble young man, Petey will fix you right up, won't you Petey." Ms. Barbara stammers.

With that, this big doo-fuss-looking fucker comes towards me and the car with a big ass fireman's house, spraying the car. Jumping out of the way, running and waving for Petey not to do that, I was stopped by a not-so-feeble-looking Ms. Ann. Her death grip on my shoulder hurts like shit, then slowly she releases me.

"What are you people talking about!? I was leaving for work assholes!" I said, turning away from Ms. Ann, as I'm holding my pained shoulder.

"No, you weren't," Charles said, matter-of-factly.

"We know everything young man, we know everything," Mr. P. Pye exhorts.

"Let me tell you another thing you don't know but it's time you did," He continues.

"You are what we've been waiting for years. You can never leave. We made grave miscalculations when your ancestors left. The Master promised us that when another Middleort moved back into Acer Hill, they will keep them here forever."

Mr. P.Pye points to the thousands of big black birds now draped over my house and my surrounding trees.

"They'll keep YOU, our new evil element here forever. Evil was dormant while you were here. Master was preparing us to assist you in guiding us as we spread a more generous evil throughout the city of Baltimore and beyond. Welcome Home."

# PIECES OF A DREAM

Sizzling. The pig is roasting over an open fire, turning over and over. With each turn, the hellfire pulls more life out of the already dead animal. Scottie sits there watching. Waiting for his turn and Leroy, his Pa's, approval, to do 'the dance'. That's what Scottie calls the slaughtering of the pig by Pa. Large ax, pig squealing mercifully for help, blood splattering everywhere and Pa having that satisfied look on his face. Like doing the ho-down with Ma is what Pa said, hence 'the dance'. This is all-natural to Scottie. He'd watch his Pa slaughter many animals but a pig killing made Pa very happy. Scottie wants that happiness. Scottie wants to use the axe. His Ma told Pa that letting Scottie watch the slaughtering was unhealthy for a child his age, but Pa said it'll help Scottie become a 'man'.

Seven years have passed on. Ma had passed earlier that Summer and Scottie was becoming a man. Sandy's blonde hair chiseled strong face with matching body and an intelligence most farm boys would crave for. Physically he was becoming a man but to his Pa he was still a boy. Every chore Scottie did except one, 'the dance.' He wanted to do 'the dance' badly.

The passing of Ma hurt Scottie a lot but he found comfort in Lucy. She lived on the farm five miles down the road. They spent a great deal of time together for she reminded him a lot of his Ma. Short stocky build, cherub beautiful face, dark frizzled hair, and a sweet enduring smile. They've been friends for 17 years, enjoying their skinny dipping at Butch Creek, racing down Boskent Lane and the occasional 'hay gathering'. That's what they both called sex. They also loved playing games. There was this one particular game they really enjoyed. At Butch Creek, at their secret spot, Lucy would act out 'the dance'. Scottie would take a large stick and start wailing away with it towards Lucy who was acting like she was a pig. Squealing, snorting, and prancing around on her hands and knees. Scottie took great care not to swing too close to Lucy but she didn't mind because she knew afterward 'hay gathering' was going to happen.

As the summer's coming to a close, Scottie is still doing his normal chores, watching Pa doing 'the dance' and 'hay gathering' with Lucy. He also was preparing for his last year in High School. With all that he was enduring, Scottie was doing very well in school and being considered for an academic scholarship from the university in the city.

"Come here boy!" Pa yells.

Leaving his room, Scottie sees Pa standing in front of the barn. The morning sun emphasized the years of hard work entrenched in Pa's unwrinkled face, just lines of worry and pain. Pa's a sinewy strong man, wearing a dirty red University of Wisconsin t-shirt under overalls stained with years of pig blood and dirt. In his tapered withered left hand he holds the axe. The one he does 'the dance' with.

"Shit. I guess he wants me to watch the last 'dance' of the summer," Scottie mutters.

Pa squints his eyes, spits tobacco from his tight mouth.

"Tomorrow boy, you do 'the dance'."

After saying this, Pa turns and goes back into the barn. Scottie stands there in disbelief. Then it hits him.

"'The dance', 'the dance'!!" Scottie yells, running up the road to tell Lucy.

Once there he's smiling and fidgeting profusely as he tells Lucy what his Pa tells him.

"I've got to practice. Make him and Ma proud of me." Scottie said, kissing Lucy on her lips, neck and shoulder.

"Fine honey, let's go practice now then some 'hay gathering'." Lucy coos, while fondling his crotch.

"Yeah, we'll practice, but it's got to be special, very special. Just wait till tonight Lucy. Wait till tonight."

Later that night, Scottie and Lucy head up to Butch Creek.

"What's in the bag Scottie?" Lucy asked, looking at the tan burlap bag in his hands.

"Something special for the practice."

"Ooooo....sounds good."

Arriving at their spot, Lucy lunges at Scotties crotch.

"Not yet. Calm down!"

Very disappointed, Lucy walks away from Scottie and begins doing what she literally came to do, act the role of a pig.

"What are you waiting for?" Lucy asked, while on her hands and knees, awaiting Scottie's actions. He just stands there, with a hand in the burlap bag.

"Well!?"

Scottie pulls his hand from the burlap bag. Attached to his right hand is a thick black axe handle with the words 'MA' carved in red paint. The axe head itself has a bolt of lightning engraved on it.

"Wait a minute. What the hell you 'bout to do with that?" Lucy asked, getting up as quickly as her portly body would let her.

"Shit Lucy. You think I'm going to chop you up or something. I just gotta get used to the weight of this axe as I swing it. Nowhere near you. I promise."

Very reluctant, Lucy gets back on her hands and knees, watching closely as the axe swings near her body but not close enough to be hit. After a few swings, her prancing around got more intense, rumbling around moving further away from the sharp pendulum. In making a quick move to her left, Lucy's knee strikes a shedded porcupine quill forcing her sharpley to the right. Right under Scottie's Thor-like movement of his axe to her left arm. Yelping in extreme pain, Lucy grabs for her shoulder and pierced knee, falling heavy to the ground.

"Asshole! You cut me!"

Standing there in somewhat shock, Scottie couldn't believe he hit her with the axe. All at once a strange eerie warm sensation caresses his body.

"This must be what Pa feels when he does 'the dance'." Scottie said to himself.

Wanting more, he lowers his left arm to help Lucy up, he stops and strikes another blow with the axe to her back.

"What the fuck!!!" Lucy screams.

Methodical and harsh, Scottie places crashing blows to her body. It feels great to him. With each blow comes the thudding crunch of steel on flesh then steel on bone, producing squirts and flumes of blood. Lucy's writhing in pain. Scottie with a satisfied feeling sweeping his body.

"'The dance'. 'The dance '. Yes! Yes! 'The dance'!" Scottie yells, as his blows become piston-like on Lucy's body.

"Yo Scottie. You ready!?"

Brian, Scottie's college roommate. He was yelling at Scottie to wake up for his morning class.

"You look like shit," Brian said, collecting his books.

"Bad dream." Scottie mumbles.

For the past year since Lucy's death, Scottie had nightmares almost every night about the incident at Butch's Creek. Those nightmares bothered him a great deal but he couldn't tell anyone about them. Especially since Lucy was written off as a missing person, not a person found in the meat grinder for pig food.

Going to class, Scottie refused to let the nightmares affect his school life. He had too much going on at the time. Away from home for the first time, away at college and Jannie. She and Scottie meant during Freshman Orientation. They spent tons of time together, but they were never intimate. Scottie didn't attempt anything on purpose because Jannie resembles Lucy. He thought many times to put an end to their platonic relationship but somehow talking to her soothed him.

That day turned out to be typical for Scottie. Nothing was out of wack. He's to meet Jannie for dinner at the Badger Inn to relax. Jannie beats him there so she waits patiently.

Fifteen minutes later, Scottie shows up.

"'Bout time you got here."

"Sorry. I had to talk to Dr. Sterling after class." Scottie said, placing a peck on Jannie's cheek.

During dinner, Scottie wondered if he hung out all night with Jannie would he have nightmares about Lucy. He wished that he could really talk to Jannie about what's happening to him. As they're leaving the Badger Inn, Jannie turns to Scottie.

"Are you going to the dance?" she asked.

"Dance? What dance?"

"You know, the dance this Friday at the Hen House."

"Oh, that dance. Sure, but I need a date," he said, drawing a smile on his tight face.

"Well, you have two days to get one sweetheart," she said, tickling his ribs.

That night, Scottie and Brian are in their room studying.

"I'm calling it quits dude," Brian says, flopping onto his bed.

Scottie never said a word nor moved an inch. He was deep into his studying and afraid to go to sleep. The clock read 1:00 am. Scottie knew he had an early class tomorrow, but he decided to try and stay up all night to avoid the nightmare. He had tried that several times in the past, sometimes he was able to, other times he couldn't. It was a noble effort, but Scottie fell asleep in his chair, upright, with his head cocked backwards.

A dull thud. Then a resounding crunch. Lucy's severed arm lay on Butch's Creek shore. Her fingers were wiggling as waves of blood caresses its bicep and forearm. Another dull thud. The other arm. This one just lay there with its fingers balled up into a bloody fist. Scottie has a satisfied look carved into his face. It felt great. Maybe too great.

"Dammit sleepy head! Time to get up!" Brian, once again, was yelling to wake Scottie.

"Wow. Studying kicked my ass last night. More reason for me not to do it."

"Whatever dude. I hope you make your 8:45 am class." Brian said, leaving the room.

The clock reads 8:30 am. Scottie jumps up from the chair grabs his books and rushes out the door. When he made it to class all he could think about was last night's nightmare. Hard for him to think of anything else. He had better luck with the next few classes. Less nightmare, more classwork. Later that afternoon he runs into Jannie.

"Don't forget the dance tomorrow," she said.

"Don't call it that. Call it a mixer, party, a get-together. Anything but the damned dance. That sounds so juvenile!" Scottie said, in a hot-tempered fashion.

"Well excuse the hell out of me for being juvenile."

"Baby I'm sorry. I didn't mean for it to sound that way. I was just joking." Scottie said, pretty upset the nightmare was getting the best of him.

Late that night, Scottie was once again trying to stay up all night by watching television. Too many things are sprinting through his mind; tomorrow's party, the nightmares, and what he said to Jannie earlier. All this however made his brain and body more weary. Slowly he dozes off.

Repetitive pounding. Lucy's legs are tough to sever. That healthy farm girl girth made it harder than the arms. With anxiety, Scottie heaves the axe mightily into her legs. Blood geysers from her veins onto Scottie and Mother Earth. Smiling because one leg was finally severed. He watches her femur slowly poke out from her leg stump as if it's searching the twilight for its enemy. Scottie was satisfied.

"Hey man! I can't be doing this shit every morning!" Brian yells, shaking Scottie's shoulders.

"Yeah, yeah. Ok, thanks man. I promise this won't happen again." Scottie said, hedging to the bathroom.

He knows he needs help and someone to talk to but he can't risk it. All he can do is try harder to control the nightmares.

Friday night. Scottie escorts Janinie to the dance. The music, the adult drinks and holding onto Jannie's firm body didn't help scatter the thoughts of the nightmare. After the dance, Scottie walks Jannie to her dorm. She invites him up. Inside her room Jannie closes the door and holds Scottie's hand.

"Scottie. We've been together for a short time. I really really like you...."

"I like you too Lucy..."

"...No, let me finish. I don't get to see much of you, but when I do, I just want to kiss you all over. Tonight, I will." Lucy said, kissing Scottie passionately while rubbing his crotch.

He was very surprised since their kissing had never gone this far. Scottie figured this may help him clear his mind of the nightmares.

Falling to the floor in an explosive passionate embrace, Jannie pushes her tongue into Scottie's hungry mouth. After a few minutes, Jannie pulls away.

"I have a great surprise for you. I hope you can handle it."

Jannie has no roommate so there's no need to worry about any intrusion.

"I'll be right back," Jannie said, carrying a medium-size blue box into the bathroom with her.

Scottie starts ripping off what's left of his clothes, pulls back the covers, and jumps into the bed. The bathroom door creaks open. Scottie lays there, mesmerized by Jannie's naked body, except for a red leather motorcycle cap and red leather gloves. Her left hand holds a black rubber night-stick. Puzzled, but very interested, Scottie opens up the covers.

"I like things, different. I hope this doesn't frighten you?" Jannie said.

"Naw, different is good."

"Take this. I've been a naughty girl and I need a spanking" she said, handing Scottie the night-stick.

Firmly, Scottie strikes the night-stick across her ass.

"Harder!" Jannie moans.

Doing as he was told, Scottie places a blacksmith-type blow to her ass.

"Yes." she hums.

Scottie continues her flogging. With each blow comes mini flashbacks of Lucy popping in his head. The crunching bones. The blood jetting out. The synchronicity of his blows. The look on Lucy's face. The satisfied look on his. On Jannie's desk next to her bed are a large pair of shearing scissors. Instinctively Scottie grabs them.

"'The dance!' 'The dance!'" Scottie blusters from his lungs.

# OUIJA

"What's this shit!!"

"Ooohhhh! Daddy, you cussed us!" We all said, in unison.

"Answer me dammit!! What is this shit!!"

Daddy is talking about the board game me and my sisters, Kelly and Ian are playing. It's a stupid phony game to us, something called Ouija. We place our fingertips on this elevated game piece with a glass window. We ask a question and the windowed game piece is supposed to slide to the words "yes" or "no" or spell out words from the alphabet on the game board. At least that's what the instructions read. We found it in Aunt Vi's closet. I'm, Deany, the oldest at 11. Kelly is 9 and Ian is 8. With sheer shock and confusion, we watch daddy frantically grab the game board, the elevated game piece and throw them into the game box. He stares at us with his old man nose opening wide and his burning eyes.

"Deany, where did you get this from!?" Daddy asks, softening his voice.

You see, I'm always sick. Going back and forth to my doctor and hospital because of this disease. It's this thing that won't let me breathe right. As always, like my shows on PBS and the many books I read, I play to my audience.

"Aunt Vi's closet," I said, coughing and slightly wheezing.

Daddy's temper eases some more. He had already placed the items in the box. He turns, storming towards the kitchen. Kelly and Ian are now crying. Motioning for them to stop, I watch daddy take the board game out to the backyard. He cracks the box and board game in two with his bare hands. He then stomps on the elevated game piece several times. Afterwards, all broken pieces are placed in the tin trashcan. Just then Aunt Vi walks through the front door.

"What's wrong with you two?" Aunt Vi asks.

"Daddy cussed at us!" Kelly and Ian sobbingly yell.

"What?"

Aunt Vi then looks at me standing in the kitchen.

"What are you doing Deany?"

Saying nothing, I point to the kitchen door. Aunt Vi walks in and sees daddy coming up the back porch steps, fuming. Before he could reach the door, Aunt Vi rushed by me.

"Why in the hell did you cuss at the children Mr. Christian man!?"

Daddy stops at the top of the steps with his old man nose opening wider. His voice is low, grumbly, and direct.

"You had that God-forsaken game in my Catholic house. You made me use foul language to my children. You are one step to being thrown out of my house."

"That game is harmless and fun. Me, Tina and Quinnie play with it all the time, especially when you ain't here."

"You and your sisters won't be fooling with that nonsense anymore. I broke it and trashed it."

Aunt Vi knew she was licked. Huffing, she turns away from daddy and slaps me upside my head before running to her room. I start wailing and crying my eyes out until I see daddy unbuckling his belt. Causing me to haul ass out of there, followed by Kelly and Ian.

Later that evening, daddy had a family meeting with our ma, Aunt Vi and Aunt Tina. Us children were told to stay upstairs in our room with the television. Of course, my nosy ass sat on the top step, listening. I couldn't hear too much but I did hear something like, 'this is a Catholic house', 'how dare they defy his wishes', and 'they've sinned.' My eavesdropping was going unnoticed until I have a coughing attack. My mother runs to the steps with my vaporizer in her hand. Once again, I played to my audience.

"I was coming to get my thing from you. I felt an attack coming." I wheeze to ma, daddy and my aunts. Behind me are my sisters with Ian also holding a vaporizer.

After my episode, I hear Aunt Vi apologize to daddy. They all say a prayer then ma and Aunt Vi come upstairs for bed. Aunt Tina leaves to go to her little apartment. Daddy stays downstairs, watching the late news. I ease myself down there to be with him.

"Who won daddy?"

"Sports hasn't come on yet."

"Oh. I'm sorry about today. We didn't mean to make you mad."

"You didn't know the evil behind that game. You all know now and I'm satisfied. I too apologize for cursing at you all. Sports is on boy."

We both groan as the sports announcer report that the Orioles lost against the Brewers.

"Oh well. Time for you to go to sleep boy."

"Ok. Good night daddy."

In the morning, everything was sort of back to normal. My sisters' clothes, as well as mine, are laid out at the bottom of the bed for school. The fresh smell of cheesy eggs, bacon, pan-fried potatoes, and scrapple jitterbug up our noses. I finish washing up and scurry downstairs with Kelly and Ian for breakfast.

"Deany! Stop running!" Daddy yells.

Slowing down, I quickly walk to the table. Ma and Aunt Vi have already eaten and left for work.

That evening, I'm doing an art homework assignment and I need a pair of scissors. I know there are none in my room, so I go to Aunt Vi.

"Aunt Vi. Do you have any scissors?"

"Yeah boy. In the closet," she said, while painting her nails.

The clutter in her closet is unbelievable. I have to fight through all this crap to find some stupid scissors. There is so much to fight through, old clothes, shoes, stockings, books and shoeboxes of letters. My curiosity wants to know what's in these letters. As I start to take a letter out of its envelope, I see the stupid scissors and it. The Ouija board game box. At first, I just stare at the game. Imagining Aunt Vi going out and buying another game to piss off daddy. That thought was just crazy. Maybe her and ma pulled it from the trash, but it was all broken up by daddy. Plus, the trashmen came this morning.

"Aunt Vi?"

"Yeah?"

I want to ask her about the Ouija board game but I chicken out.

"Nothing. I found them." I said, quickly wrapping a towel around the board game, rushing out of the room.

"No running with scissors boy!" Aunt Vi yells, never turning her head from painting her nails.

Luckily, Kelly and Ian weren't in our bedroom when I came in with the stuff. I quickly slide the covered board game under my part of the bed and started cutting up designs for my homework art project. The whole time I'm wondering how that game made it back into our house.

Almost time for my sister's bedtime. They, along with ma, had come into the bedroom an hour ago. I've finished my project and ma was helping with Kelly's homework. The three of us sleep in this room. Full-size bed, medium burnt wood dresser, a rickety wire tv stand, a dusty no remote tv and a large scary weird white dingy polar bear-looking wardrobe.

"Deany. Let me see your project." ma said.

Showing it to her, hoping she approves then leaves right away, I almost rip my project in half, being fast.

"Boy slow down. Shit."

"Sorry, ma."

"Nice. You do real nice work on your art." ma said, inspecting my art homework.

"Thank you, ma."

"Now y'all get ready for bed."

We did our normal routine before bed. Put on our pajamas, brush our teeth, my sisters tie up their hair and we goof around until ma comes back in our room. She makes sure we're under the covers then kisses us 'goodnight' and leaves. It was killing me. I'm so anxious to show Kelly and Ian what I found in Aunt Vi's closet but I have to make sure ma ain't coming back in.

"Hey. I got something to show y'all but y'all gotta promise me to be real quiet. Especially you Kelly. This is a big huge secret so be cool and quiet when y'all see it."

"Yeah, yeah. Hurry up, boy. I'm sleepy." Ian said.

I remove my blanket showing them both the game.

"Oooooh Deany. You gonna get it!" Kelly shouts.

"Girl shut the hell up before I pop you." I angrily whispered.

A few seconds go by and we don't hear any yelling or fussing coming from ma or daddy.

"Why you take that outta the trash can?" Ian asks.

"I didn't. I found it in Aunt Vi's closet. Maybe she took it from the trash can."

"Then she gonna be in trouble too." Kelly said.

"Yeah, probably. Let's play the game tonight before I put it back in Aunt Vi's closet."

"Ok. But be real quiet." Kelly said, sarcastically.

"Daddy broke the game board remember," Ian said.

Kelly and I both frown at Ian as I slowly open the box. The board game itself is not broken nor is that elevated piece. I shrug my shoulders and pull the game board out. Kelly and Ian already have their fingertips on the elevated game piece. I place mine on it too.

"Who's the evil person in this house? I ask.

Within seconds the elevated game piece begins to move. Ian giggles as Kelly's eyes bug out in fright yet she manages to stay connected to the elevated piece. She's probably too scared to take them off. The elevated piece slowly moves towards the letter "Y" then quickly to the letters "O" and "U".

"You!" Kelly shouts.

"What the heck are you kids doing in there!?" daddy shouts.

"Nothing daddy!" I yell while covering the mouths of Kelly and Ian.

"Go to sleep! Now!" daddy yells.

Removing my hands from their mouths, Kelly gives me the evil eye stare.

"Why did you ask that stupid question?" Kelly asks.

"'Cause I wanted to know if it was daddy."

"Well, it's you, dummy," Ian said.

"But I ain't evil."

"The game says you is. You're the one that set the house on fire. You killed our doggy. You cooked our pet fish in the frying pan. You pushed down Aunt Tina when she was sick. And everyone knows you broke old lady Ms. Barbara's leg by tripping her." Kelly said.

"To hell with you Kelly."

"Not me evil boy, you."

Early that morning, after Aunt Vi left her room to shower, I'm sneaking the game back into her closet. Suddenly I start wheezing. Within an instant I can't breathe, my chest is tight and my body goes numb. Last thing I remember is falling hard against

the wall and the Ouija game falls from my hands.

Groggy, lost and scared. I wake up in a place that ain't home. Things are bright and clean, but I see ma, daddy and Aunt Tina through my fog.

"There he is. Hi baby. How you feel?" ma asks, hovering over me.

"Ma? I'm okay. Asthma attack?"

"Yeah boy, a big one too. God knows I'm happy you're ok. Prayed greatly for you boy. Even though you were found with that sinful game in your hands. Where in God's name did you....."

"Jim. Not now. Please." ma said.

Daddy looks very upset that ma told him to stop.

"I'm leaving. I'm taking that game to the basement and burn it in the furnace. Burning it back to hell." daddy said, leaving the room in a huff.

"Real crazy shit at your house." Aunt Tina said.

That night, after they left, I lay in bed thinking. 'Why did that game say I am the evil one in the house?'

At the house, Deany's father, as true a real Christian man as there is, makes his wife, their daughters and his two sisters-in-law witness him throwing the Ouija board game into the coal-burning furnace. He places more coal in the furnace to make it hotter. Unbeknownst to the family, for some strange reason Deany begins to code. While inside the furnace the game box, the board and that elevated piece crack, blister, burn and smolder. Deany wheezes, gags, thrashes about searching for air. The hospital staff try desperately to help him but they fail. Suddenly, at the house, the landline, Deany's mother and father's cell phone ring at the same time. Interrupting the last pieces of game board floating away in ashes.

"Oh MY GOD! We've got to go to the hospital now!" ma screams.

Deany's death was an extreme shock to the family and the hospital staff. They're at the hospital trying to understand, justify, validate, pray and condemn what just happened. With nothing more to do at the hospital, they all go home.

Jim exhales deeply while opening the front door of the house. Upon entry, there's the tangy smell of burning cardboard and plastic, stagnant in the air.

"Jim, open some windows please," Quinnie said, solemnly.

He rushes to the dining room to do so but stops dead in his tracks at the dining room entrance. Unexpectantly there's a God-fearing unholy scream coming from Jim. The whole family rushes to Jim's side. They witness the ghastly sight of a bloated purple Deany standing with an intact yet smoldering Ouija board game in his swelled arms.

"Evil always comes back!" Deany bellows.

# MOMMA

Askew, bloodied and dreadfully noticeable. Dawn's head is literally coming off its organic hinge. Pierre, her brother, is annoying me immensely with his herky-jerky chaotic finger pointing at her. Maxe, my darling husband, is staring deeply at me, as prescribed. Craving every movement I make.

"Enough!" I yell, slamming my fork onto the table.

Pierre stops his unrest in mid motion. One finger after another tries desperately to gather themselves. Maxe's body spasms with excitement, awaiting more anger from me. Dawn stayed still. Wide eyed, with this incredulous smile on her tilted face.

"Maxe. Pierre. Leave me. Now!"

They both bow their heads as they remove their soulless bodies from the dinner table. With stilt walker precision, they walk out of the room. Dawn attempts to follow. She tries to turn her head in their direction, but she can't. I've already clasped her chin with my hand. Tying her blood-stained napkin from her chin to the rear of her head.

"Momma!?"

"Shhhh baby. I've got to fix you."

It's been a whole year since the car accident in Kabare' in The Democratic Republic Of Congo. I was there with my family for a conference and seminar on terraforming. I'm Amanda Nortis, a Nobel Prize winning Astrophysicist from Maryland. The lead scientist on an international team. We have created a device that can terraform any planet within our galaxey without any complications or consequences.

My speech at the seminar was to inform and show the world that we have diminished all bugs and issues. The device works.

That day, the beginning anyway, was great. During the seminar my team and I received glowing accolades and praise. Supporters with monetary donations came in droves. Maxe was with the children taking in the sights of the Motherland. They were meeting me afterwards so that I too can take in the beautiful sights of Afrika. I remember telling Maxe that no matter the outcome of the seminar, I was still accompanying them.

"Hi honey. Your smile gives a glow to your body. Everything must have gone very well." Maxe said, before kissing me.

"Oh sweetheart. It went well beyond my imagination. Ninety percent of the Afrikan nations are giving their full support, money and resources. The United States, Canada, Iran, Iraq, China, Japan, Great Britain, Australia, India and all of South America are in full support. Hell, even both Koreas." I recall saying, as I wipe blood off of Dawn's neck, chin and shoulder.

My poor sweet Dawn. She doesn't talk much now. That pure enthusiasm of learning new things has dwindled. I miss the old Dawn.

"Cool beans mommy!" Did you know this area of Afrika gets 205.31 strikes of lightning per 247 acres every year and Lake Kivu is 56 miles long and 31 miles wide…." Dawn excitedly said, before being cut off by Pierre.

"THIS food here is funny looking!" Pierre whines.

"I wasn't finished square poot!" Dawn yells.

That day was fun, electric, exhilarating and quite fulfilling. Echoing back to that day, I calmed them both down very quickly. Maxe, as usual, was trying to discipline quietly but no one heard him. Feeling it was time to get my kids out of there, I bid goodbyes to my colleagues, supporters and my team. According to Maxe we're going to a village on the shores of Lake Kivu.

He was driving. I was enjoying the beautiful weather, the rays of the sun and the smell of exotic botany waffling through my nose. Without warning, as though we've angered the gods. Multiple bolts of lightning strike our car and the road. Bright hot flashes of light, burning metal, flying asphalt and tons of flying dust distort us all. I see Dawn and Pierre in the distance. For some reason I'm nowhere near the car. They're both lying next to one another by what's left of the car. I can make out that Pierre was raising his head and opening his mouth over and over but it's entombed with blood. If he was saying anything or making noises I couldn't tell because I couldn't hear anything. I could tell he was in pain but I couldn't tell the level. Dawn's level I could tell. Her head was no longer connected to her body.

Just thinking about that horrible day has me shaking as I stitch the fishing wire tighter to Dawn's neck and the top portion of her back. Seeing my babies like that was complete torture. Getting myself off the ground, I wobbled through the large pieces of flaming asphalt and smoking car pieces to get to my children.

Getting to Pierre first, I grabbed hold of him and turned him away from the mortality of his sister.

"Maxe! Where is Maxe!?" I began screaming, but I need to tend to my child.

In helping him to get to his feet to get away from the burning car, Pierre frantically jerked his arms and body. His face contorted harshly like he was having a stroke. Still not able to hear, I saw him wildly pointing to his legs. They were both gone. Bloody shredded stumps below his knee.

Composing myself as best I could, I lifted Pierre up, carrying him to a safe distance from the car. I managed to wrap Pierres wounds to stop the blood. Now to find Maxe. I make my way back over to the burning car. Standing over Dawn, I bend down to move her too when through the smoke and erratic sparks I see Maxe. Like me, he was thrown from the car. He was laying face down on his stomach, motionless. Leaving Dawn, I make it to Maxe. He was in one piece with no visible blood. Cautiously, I slowly turn him over. His chest, that beautiful impressive chest, was crushed inward. There was blood, not much. That was caused by his ribs and sternum protruding through his beautiful Black skin. Maxe released a harsh breath. I waited for a return breath but none came. In the distance amidst the chaos, I see the flashing lights of EMT vehicles.

Weeks after my recovery and release from the hospital, I was given a quaint beautiful cottage that sat alone next to a small pond. The Institute, the company I work for, supplied it. They also arranged a live-in nurse. That lasted a few days as did my tolerance for my colleagues and team members visiting daily. I just wasn't ready to be around anyone besides my family, whom I still have to bury.

I wanted to have the traditional wake at the cottage. The Institute arranged for their bodies and coffins to be delivered to me. They were placed in the garage next to the cottage. After their delivery I logged off my mind. Chamomile tea and a sci-fi movie comforted me. The movie was about terraforming a planet. As the movie was ending, charges of crazy synapse go off within my head.

"Terraforming..... I wonder."

Instantly I telephoned my assistant Donna back home in Maryland.

"Donna."

"Amanda!? Are you ok? What's wrong?"

"Nothing darling. Nothing at all. I'm fine. I need you to go to the lab and send me the terraforming prototype."

"Send it to you? There in Afrika? Why?"

"Donna, I don't need you adding to my grief. You have my address. Just send it overnight. Thanks. Bye."

Grabbing a notepad and pen, I write down equations, formulas and thoughts regarding my using my terraforming device to bring back my family. If I can bring life to a planet, I damn sure can try to bring life to humans.

While awaiting my package from Donna, I remove my family from their coffins. Strip them of their clothes and remove all inorganic materials from the garage. It also wasn't easy, but my scientific credentials and name pulled some weight in The Congo. I was able to obtain two amputated legs cut below the knee, a tragic farming accident. A perfect beautiful female head, the result of a horrid lover's triangle gone bad and the most exquisite human torso with damaged but serviceable organs. That story I didn't ask about.

My medical knowledge helped a great deal in aligning two amputated legs to Pierre's limp stumps. The town mortician had done an excellent job on his stumps. There was a slight discoloration though. Pierre's loss of blood made him a bit lighter in color than the legs. I calculated that after the terraforming process that would change. Connecting his blood vessels, bone and cartilage was challenging. Sewing two dead body parts to one another was almost my Waterloo. What saved me were thoughts of helping my mother sewing Girl Scout uniforms for her job when I was younger. My next task is Dawn.

I marveled at the severed head of this young Afrikan girl. She looks about 16 or so, slender taught face enveloped in dark azure skin, large brown almond eyes and full enticing bloodless lips. To my surprise, connecting blood vessels, nerves and the stem weren't too difficult. The most difficult part was keeping the stem fully connected together. Strong tensile wire, surgical tape, duct tape and vaseline did the trick though. Luckily, Dawn's skin and her new head matched perfectly.

Maxe is on the dirt floor naked, upper body a jigsaw puzzle. Detached left arm was a bit off centered to the new torso it's about to receive even though the torso was set perfectly for attachments. Both arms, neck and waist are ready. My tedious mind-numbing calculations and formulas informed me that the terraforming process will add life to my husband's new internal organs. Sewing that new gorgeous torso to Maxe's bottom torso filled me with great zeal, along with the torrid passion in knowing what I'm doing is the right thing to do. With each seam and suture, I almost felt him grow warm but that was my imagination. With the lower stitches set, the arms and neck are next. Those items were a breeze. Practice from Dawn and Pierre helped. The only thing that dismayed me with Maxe were his cadaverous dark eye sockets. A result of being struck in the chest by two lightning bolts.

All three were now ready. One more check of the garage for any inorganic materials removal was taken. I laid their naked bodies six feet apart. Not sure why, I guess all those past years of social distancing were embedded in my framework. Everything was set. I placed my terraforming prototype next to the garage door, kissed each of my baby's, ran to my prototype, pushed the button and rushed out the door. A brilliant light belched out of my device. Even with the dark goggles on I turned my head away from the garage. With unexpected vigor, a large bolt of lightning struck an unnoticed small lightning rod atop the garage. I remember screaming to the top of my lungs, "No!" Flashing was still going on, but very minimal now, but I wasn't sure if the whole process was over. Then I heard a monstrous scream coming from the garage. My eyes and heart inspirited me as I rushed to the garage door. Yanking it open, I see Dawn sitting upright at the waist, staring at her smoldering arms, yelping like a puppy. As I approached her she moaned.

"Yooouuuu."

I wasn't sure if she recognized me or was blaming me for her damnation. My thoughts of that day are very clear to me as I continue to fix Dawn. When I saw her alive that day I said, "Baby! It's me, momma."

"Momma!?"

"Yes Baby, momma. It's me, momma."

"Momma!?"

"Yes, momma."

Dawn became less excited. I truly calculated that she would speak French. The terraforming process would render her brain new to an extent and I was prepared for that. To my surprise she spoke English with a French accent in a childlike, programmable manner.

As I embraced my baby, I looked at the inactive bodies of Maxe and Pierre.

"Baby, stay here. Don't move."

As I moved away from Dawn she moved along with me and I didn't stop her. When we got closer to Maxe both of his arms started to flinch. Dawn reached out, grabbing Maxe's left arm. With that, Maxe abruptly sat up smiling broadly with his cheek bones pushing heavily against his settled eye sockets. Not saying a word, he and Dawn embraced and didn't let go. That gave me a chance to check on Pierre. He was still inanimate. I whispered into his ear, "Pierre." Nothing. I said his name louder, no response. Surprisingly, Dawn, still embracing Maxe, screamed out Pierre's name.

"PIERRE!"

"Shit! My legs hurt!" Pierre blurts.

"Oh my baby." I said to Pierre.

"I baby! Not that!" screamed Dawn, pointing at Pierre.

Those days were trying to say the least. Teach, discipline and fight basically three new children. Right now I'm almost done fixing Dawn's head. This has occurred several times before. Each time I think I've completely fixed her, but I'm missing something. As long as my baby is alive I don't care.

The following morning there's a knock at my door. I know who it is, it's Maxe. Every morning for the last year, he knocks on my bedroom door to get the 'ok' to enter. He and the children sleep in the garage, they truly enjoy each other's company. Sometimes I feel like an afterthought.

"Come in Maxe!"

He enters with his usual huge smile and a thick black heavy wooden pick in his left hand, motioning it in a combing way. Smiling at my husband, I motion for him to come to me. His smile grows wider as his cybernetic movements of his upper torso enable him to meander my way. Maxe stands directly in front and begins to pick my medium length bush. His pick strokes are very gentle, serene, and loving. Leaning forward, I kiss my husband. His somber concave eyes perk up. Perversely he starts unbuttoning his pants.

"No!" I scream, pulling his hands back up to my hair.

Maxe glares at me with what looks like slight malice in those desolate eyes as he continues picking my hair. I'm not feeling his reception to my stopping his sexual movement, plus I hear the children entering the other room turning on the television.

"Leave me Maxe."

Closing his worn eyes, he exhales deeply before leaving. The children are happy to see Maxe as I see them joyously patting him on his arms and chest. I didn't know what to think about Maxe's reaction to my ordering him to stop his sexula advance and picking of my hair. Usually when I tell him to stop, he does it without remorse. Just more things I had to indulge myself with along with how long can I keep my family hidden from the public. A few days ago I was informed by The Institute that my time in the cottage was nearing its end. My stalling and lame excuses to stay were tiring me out.

"Momma. Come look, come look." Dawn said.

"Just a second baby."

Going into the other room, I see the three of them are watching a horror movie. This, I find very strange and inappropriate for this time of the morning.

Leaping in front of them, I turn off the television.

"Momma you different. Much different than me, daddy and this thing."

"No baby. I'm not different from you three." I said, with my back still facing the three on the sofa.

I can see the three of them on the sofa through the turned off television screen. Dawn is holding a small scythe. Turning slowly to face them, I see Maxe is holding that black heavy wooden pick. Pierre is weaponless.

"Dawn!? What's that in your hand!?"

"Something to prove you not like us."

Springing fast from the sofa, Dawn embeds the scythe into my throat. Manically, I reach for her arms, pushing them away from me, instinctively pulling out the scythe. I see and feel my blood torrent from my body. Through my shock and delirium I now feel the dull sharp burning pain of Maxe gorging me with that infernal pick. My last bit of consciousness sees Pierre standing there, dumbfounded. Maybe he'll save me. But I quickly realized that his look of astonishment was not due to my plight but the fact that he had nothing to help his father and his sister. My true terror climaxees when I see Pierre rip one of his legs off to bludgeon my already dying body.

# BLACK, WHITE, AND BLOOD RED ALL OVER

Stephan's athleticism, beauty, humor, articulation of English, French, Spanish and the Cantonese language is a great catch for any woman. He had attended the oldest Historically Black College and University, Jona State, 45 miles outside of Philadelphia, Pennsylvania. He was there for two years but had to transfer to Frip University, a large white, very white, school in Arizona. His military dad was relocated and his mom was very concerned about leaving her baby in Pennsylvania.

There are some Black students at Frip U. However, it seems that the few dwindle into less each day. Stephan didn't think the change would alter his life too much. Too bad he couldn't see into the future.

The start of the Fall semester. In Dr. Taylor's Rhetorical Theory class sits Stephan. The lone Black sitting in that sea of white. Resembling that bug smashed upon a car window, messing up the clarity. Stephan's reaching for the class syllabus when she walks in. Medium length Raven black hair, a dancer's figure and a sweet but I'll kick your ass flow to her. Everyone, women too, were checking her out. Some with contempt because she's interrupting the start of class others googling her with lust. She's a white girl but damn she's fine.

The only seat left is the one next to Stephan's right. Passing by him to get by she steps on his foot.

"Oh shit. I'm so sorry." she said, catching her balance.

"Clumsy little...."

"Sophia to you, mister."

Stephan stares at her in amazement and anger.

"Can we settle down now that Miss Songria has joined us!?" Dr. Taylor said, trying to ease the tension.

Interesting introduction by the two. The fun was just beginning.

It's now the middle of the semester, mid-terms approaching. Stephan's in the Student Union game room playing a video game. Sophia walks in carrying a video camera case, a tripod and her briefcase. Fumbling and clutching her equipment, she looks straight at Stephan. He ignores her.

"What an asshole. He's not even trying to help or anything." Sophia says to herself.

He thought about it for a second, but that was it, a second of "hell no."

"Can you give me a hand!?"

Stephan looks around the game room to see if anyone else was there but he's alone with her.

"Who, me? Can't you see my ass is busy."

Her eyes twinge as she huffs away, dropping then dragging her equipment. Minutes later Stephan came to his senses. Realizing what he did was rude and ignorant, he left the video game to apologize and help. Through the glass doors of the Student Union there she is, still fumbling with the equipment. He sees that her mouth is moving a mile a minute, like she's cussing someone out but there's no one around. Giggling, Stephan removes the glass obstacle barrier but hurridely returns back to the cool comfort. That Arizona heat hit him upside his head like a heavyweight blindside punch. Standing there watching the poor girl struggle, Stephan relents and goes to her aid. By now Sophia was just dragging the tripod, its metal scratching was reminiscent of a Lion's paw stopping his entrance into the cage. Just as the briefcase was falling from her arms Stephan caught it. For a split second they just stare at one another.

"What the fuck do you want!?"

"Damn, just trying to help."

"I don't need your help now!"

"I'm sorry, for real. I'm having mid-term pressure. Slap me if you like."

The entire time Stephan's apologizing Sophia wasn't listening. Her attention was in Stephan's strong cheek lines in his beautiful Black face, the way the sweat glistened off his body, the sensual motion of his lips when he speaks and that damned sparkle in his eyes. People in the quad are staring at them but neither notice.

"Here, let me carry the tripod and camera case." Stephan said, reaching for the tripod.

"Sure. Take it then."

"Damn, this shit is heavy. How'd you make it this far in this heat? Work out much?"

"Yeah, enough to kick your ass if need be."

"No need for violence. By the way, I'm…."

"Yeah I know, Stephan Omar Carriff."

"What!? You're a stalker or IRS Agent?"

They both smile. Stephan's impressed but he's one of the few Black men on campus and they do share a class.

The sun's heat is piercing their skin but in their weird new bliss they were impervious to its pain. They were also oblivious to the cocked lunch-time eyes beaming at them from the cafeteria's large windows as they walked by. Some stare in wonderment, some in anger.

During their walk they were both surprised and pleased how easy it was to talk to one another, although horrible stereotypes ran through each head they silently concluded they were attracted to one another.

"Here we are." Sophia said.

Stephan stops, looks up and sees that they're in front of her dorm. They walk in awaiting the elevator. Their talking and laughing continues until the elevator door opens. Two white guys are on the elevator, standing there, staring at Sophia and Stephan.

"Let me help you with that babe." one guy drawls, reaching towards Sophia.

"I've got my help!" Sophia said, pulling away.

Both white guys then look towards Stephan. Their eyes were saying "this nigger boy better only take this stuff up, then leave." That's when Stephan moves between the two white guys.

"Excuse us gents."

"Yeah, excuse you." one of the white guys snarls.

Sophia follows right behind Stephan, quickly pushing the button for her floor. The two white guys stand aside, cursing as the elevator door closes.

"Don't let that bother you Stephan."

"Already forgotten."

A faint smile crosses her face as the elevator continues to shoot upward. When they get inside the room their gabbing and joking continued. Both lost track of time and it was time for dinner. In their long conversation, feeling each other out, Stephan found out that Sophia once dated outside of her race. It didn't last though. He stated that he hadn't but felt really brave to do so if the situation permitted.

"I'm hungry. Can I join you for dinner?" he asks..

"You sure you want to do that!?" Sophia replies, with a stern hard look on her face.

"Yup."

"Ok. Before we leave I've got to find my ID." she said, kicking around her clothes on the floor.

She sees her ID under the chair Stephan is sitting in and she reaches for it. Stephan reaches for it too, crashing his head against her nose.

"Owww!! Shit!"

"Oh my God. I'm so sorry Sophia!"

"No worries." Sophia squeaks, rubbing her nose, making sure it's not bleeding.

In an instant, Stephan reaches down to peck Sophia on her nose to ease her pain. Sophia countering his move, reaching up to greet his mouth with a warm probing mouth and tongue. He lowers himself from the chair as they both grope each other, tearing at buttons and zippers. There's nothing passionate about their entanglement, all animalistic.

That night in Sophia's dorm room led to many more sexual encounters throughout the week. Friday evening, they were in her dorm room watching television when Stephan notices that Sophia is upset about something.

"Aw baby this show ain't that bad."

"Don't mind me."

"No. Tell me what's wrong." Stephan said, turning off the television.

"Just thinking about the racist people on this campus and that elevator incident."

"Baby we can handle it. Don't worry." he said, kissing her.

Sophia kisses Stephan back but her mind dwells on the 'real' problem that she just can't bear to tell him about.

"Hey baby, I just noticed your little fish aquarium is empty. What happened?"

"Oh they got sick and died."

"Wow. Sorry 'bout that. We've got to get you some new fish."

"Yeah, ok."

Sophia refused to tell him that someone poured a bottle of feminine products into the aquarium, killing the fish. She knew who did it but kept it to herself.

The next evening for dinner, Stephan and Sophia walk to the cafeteria together. She looks very nervous for some odd reason. Stephan notices. Perhaps it was what she told him yesterday about the racist eyes. He holds her closer to him. As they're standing in the food line, Sophia's inner tension goes away. She's carrying on, laughing, talking and the occasional touch of Stephan. Then suddenly Sophia blurts out.

"I've got to go! There's a girl from one of my classes who I've gotta get notes from. Bye!"

A stunned Stephan says nothing. Looking in the direction Sophia was looking he saw no one familiar. Unfortunately, that was their last encounter together.

The semester was coming to an end. Sophia's preparing for her graduation while Stephan's packing for his parents' arrival next week to take him home. Since that incident in the cafeteria the two would cross paths on campus, engaging in very small talk or the occasional nervous distant wave. While packing, Stephan checks his answering machine.

"Yo, meet me in the gym today, 7. This is Djaun, the other Black guy."

Stephan laughs, going to the next message.

"Hi honey, dad and I will be there next Friday at 11am. Be ready. Love you."

"Cool."

Walking away from the answering machine he clicks for the next message.

"Hi….how are you?"

"Oh shit, Sophia!" he yells, racing back to the answering machine.

"Life sucks, then you die. I feel like I've died. Meet me….."

Silence. Dead silence. Sophia's message wasn't finished.

"What the fuck!"

Stephan opens the answering machine and finds the tape got caught up inside.

"Old ass cheap ass machine! Fuck!"

Stephan races out of his dorm room. Dashing down the hallway to the elevator, reality hits him. What happened before is going to happen again.

"Fuck it!" Stephan yells, banging the wall, walking back to his dorm room.

Thoughts of Sophia always played in Stephan's mind in the following years. After his own graduation, a year after hers, he was hired by a local cable network. Those thoughts of Sophia began to dwindle as he became closer to his boss Tonia. A tall, athletic, fair-skinned African-American woman with a great job, great car and personality but she was going through a recent tragedy. Her husband mysteriously died and their daughter has disappeared without a trace. Her employees and Stephan did anything to ease her grief.

"Hi Stephan. What's going on?" Tonia said, in a very upbeat tone.

"Hi. You're quite chipper today. Good, I like that." he said, noticing that they're the only two in the lunchroom.

"I'm in a splendid mood today and I was thinking how nice it'd be for me to cook you dinner. I want to show you, and only you, how much I appreciate your help through my rough time." she chirped, holding and caressing his hand.

"Ummm....sure. Cool, I'm down." he said, confident but very uneasy.

He's attracted to Tonia but she is his boss, but you only live once.

"Great. Six-thirty, tonight." Tonia said, handing him a slip of paper with her address.

"Cool. I'll be there. Should I bring anything?"

"Nope."

That evening, for a very nervous man, Stephan made it through dinner without choking on his food.

"Ready for desert? It's Mississippi Mud Pie." Tonia said, going into the kitchen.

"Oh, I can't. I'm allergic to chocolate."

"I'm so sorry, I didn't know. Forgive me." she said, returning the desert to the kitchen.

"No worries. It's not your fault. Dinner was fantastic." Stephan said, trying to soothe both of their discomfort.

During dinner and conversation, Stephan's nervous probing eyes noticed that there were no pictures of Tonia's husband or daughter. 'Probably too stressful to look at', he thought. He did however notice her degree on the wall.

"You went to Frip U. I see!" he bellows toward the kitchen.

"Yeah, went there four years ago!"

"I went there too but you know that. How come you never told me you're a Frip alum?"

"Well!?" she said, sashaying from the kitchen, walking pass Stephan with two glasses and a bottle of wine into the living room.

"You had to be there when I was. There were like 10 Black students there. How'd I miss you?" he said, following her like a hungry beggar.

"You're probably right. Oh, I did mention it during your interview. Pay more attenion!" she said, with a scowl on her face.

"Well even if you were there when I was there we had to miss one another on that huge campus. Plus I stayed off campus." Stephan said, positioning himself close but not too close to Tonia on the couch.

"Yeah, big ass campus and I didn't mingle." she said, sipping her wine.

Stephan picks up his wine, sipping too. He glances at Tonia's firm looking thighs as she crosses her legs. Her dress snuggling her hips removes thoughts of Frip U, being nervous and work.

Soft music warps through the air. In a bold gesture, Stephan slowly wraps his powerful arms around Tonia's supple shoulders. Squeezing her body close to his.

"Damn...." Tonia whimpers, pulling away from his embrace, standing up.

Stephan thought she was going to change the song or something. Instead, she stands there, facing him with a weird demonic look on her face. Suddenly she begins to cry.

"My God, what's wrong. I am so sorry. I was inappropriate!" Stephan yells.

"Shhhh....I've got to tell you something." Tonia said.

"Sure, anything."

"You've been there for me, you've helped me out a great deal and without your help I may have gone crazy. But..."

"But what?" he asked, definitely thinking sex was out of the question now.

"I have to.... I have to kill you!" she yelled, smiling from ear to ear.

"What!? What'd you say?" Stephan asked, smirking and trying to draw away from her.

"You heard me dammit. You heard me well!!"

Now Stephan was trying to stand up and get away from Tonia then he realized gravity was his enemy too.

"I put a sedative in your drink. You're not going anywhere, Mr. Man!"

"Why!?" Stephan slurs.

"Why!? I'll tell you why, bitch! I knew all about that white girl you had in college." Tonia purrs.

"White girl?" Stephan gurgles.

"Yeah, white girl. Sophia Songria. Remember that message she left on your machine in college? Sophia is a real close dear friend of mine and she waited in the game room 2 long ass hours for you." Tonia said, jabbing her nails into his face.

Tonia wasn't aware that Stephan never got the full message.

"You betrayed her." Tonia whispers, getting closer to his ear lobe, biting it, drawing blood.

Grimacing in pain, there's very little Stephan can do, the sedative is almost taking over fully. He does manage to look up at Tonia as his blood oozes off the side of her mouth back to its rightful owner.

"Sophia and I were lovers. That was until you showed up. She was a stupid bitch." Tonia said, moving away from Stephan.

Sheer disbelief and bewitching horror encompses Stephan's body. He still is trying his best to get out, slumbering on the floor towards the door. He no longer could see Tonia but he can hear her from afar, yelling over and over.

"You're a man! You're a man!"

Her voice becomes clearer, indicating she's getting closer to him. Glancing ahead of him he sees Tonia's reaper shadow, holding a large meat cleaver in her hand.

"There were three things that came between me and Sophia. Looks like you're the last!"

# MY GREAT PUMPKIN

The 4.5-mile trek to the house was hard to say the least. This gigantic pumpkin Timothy found in the graveyard on Mr. LaTroi's grave kept wobbling off the rickety transport until he used his head. He took the vines off of the tree he momentarily rested on. Those vines made a good rope and they held the pumpkin in its place. Timothy first thought it was strange that there was a pumpkin in the graveyard and up-rooting it was even stranger. The harder he pulled it seemed like something or someone was pulling back. Getting nearer to the house, Timothy smells hooch cooking in the still. That meant HE was up. HE is Timothy's mother's husband, who many really didn't care for. Earl, Timothy's younger brother was up too, it was about 630 in the morning as he's finishing up his chores. Seeing Timothy and the big pumpkin, Earl hauls his ass up to greet him. Earl gazes at the pumpkin in great amazement, smiling when his brother punches him in the arm.

"Where the hell you been, you know 'lil' Earl had to do his chores and yours. I awta whip your ass Timothy. Lucky I gotta tend to the still, today's Halloween and I gotta get the hooch ready for tonite!" HE yells, walking away not noticing or paying attention to the enormous pumpkin in the wheelbarrow.

"Ma's gonna like this one." Earl said.

That's when HE saw it. HE just stares at it. Walks around it. Pokes it, then walks away, back to the still.

"Earl, help me get this in the house...." Timothy said, when thier mother came to the screen door.

She first smiles at them. Then the smile leads to jubilation as she runs down to hug the giant pumpkin.

"Glory be glory be. Timothy, where the hell did you get this from, did you steal this!" thier sneers, while poking her skinny strong hard fingers in Timothy's chest.

Drawing away from her. "No, I found it, I found it..." Timothy said, not finishing because HE came back.

"Tim boy you still here? Why ain't that thing in the house?"

Motioning to Earl, they push the wheelbarrow to the back of the house. Timothy figured since that part of the house was lower than the front it shouldn't be that hard getting the pumpkin in the kitchen. The whole time, their is just there, cuddling up next to her husband, not saying a word.

Finally, the two boys get the pumpkin into the house. Their mother comes in right behind them, going to the carving knives. She's very good at cutting, she learned it from her pa who was the best butcher in these parts. When the boy's mother starts carving the pumpkin they both witness some reddish-brown ooze slowly running down the pumpkin. She grabs a towel and wipes it off then keeps on cutting. Somehow the oozing stops.

It felt like hours to the boys but their mother had the insides of the pumpkin out and ready to make pie, mashed pumpkin potatoes and pumpkin spread which is like peanut butter in minutes. She heats the oven and places 4 pies in. Knowing it'll take about 5 to 6 hours to cook the pies. Timothy and Earl are made to go into town to get some other items for tonight. Town is about an hour and a half away. They've got to pick and buy the stuff. That'll take another hour. Treking back home depends on how heavy the stuff is or how lazy Earl gets. That can add another hour to the already hour and a half coming back. Their mother knew it would take a while. She didn't mind, nor did HE for that matter for HE was the one that gave them the money to buy the stuff.

"Can we take Barney?" Earl asked.

"Yeah, take that mutt with you. And why don't you see if anybody will buy this good for nothing coon hound!!", HE said.

Timothy loves Barney, he's the only one, besides Earl, that listens to him. When Timothy goes to the pantry to get Barney, the loyal dog looks up at him guilty. Looking around the kitchen, Timothy sees chunks of the guts of the pumpkin gone. There's pumpkin all over Barney's nose.

"Ssshhhh boy, I won't tell if you won't." Timothy said, pulling the old once reliable hound dog off the floor and scooting him out the door.

The walk to town was typical and boring. Timothy and Earl threw rocks, Barney tries to catch those rocks then he fakes chasing after squirrels, rabbits, field mice, birds and the like. They get to town, do their business and head back home. They're near Broken Knee gulch when the two boys Earl notice something's wrong with Barney. His gait is quicker than normal, and he was very, very lively, instead of almost chasing an animal he actually chased it. He too became very aggressive towards Timothy and Earl. Things came to a halt when Timothy slapped Barney on his grill to stop him from snarling at Earl. Barney glared longedly at them with blood in his eyes. His teeth, what's left of them, grit against his purple-yellow gums. The dog inched towards the boys. Timothy placed Earl behind him, the whole time backing away. Barney lunged at them releasing a nightmarish yelp. His lunge was more of a falling as his body slumped hard onto the ground. He's balled up in a knot, the demon-like sound coming from his body is scaring the bejesus out of them. Then it happened. Barney's body opens up like a ripped can of tomato sauce thrown against a huge rock. His insides are a bright orange, red color, with its insides smelling like horse shit mixed with vomit. Then it got weirder, the damned dog was trying to eat what was coming out of him. Earl and Timothy watched in horror as the dying dog was having himself as his last meal. The boys were terrified, but they got out of there, leaving their dog. It was getting later than they anticipated and were both quiet as church mice when they slowed down to a steady walk. Earl broke the silence.

"That was nasty, did you see that Timothy, ma's not gonna believe us either. Barney blew up then started eating himself."

"Be quiet Earl, we'll just tell them that Barney ran away or something...."

"You and I both know they won't believe that....I wonder what made Barney do that?"

Timothy wondered that too, then it struck him. Barney had eaten some of the pumpkin.

"Hurry up Earl, let's get home!!" Timothy yells, starting to run again.

When they got to the house there was nothing strange going on. The burned vinegar wood chip smell from the still was in the air, discarded candy wrappers were on the porch meaning some trick or treaters were there. However, they don't see or hear their mother or her husband. Timothy figures they went back into the bedroom to finish or start something.

"I want some pumpkin pie!!" Earl yells, running into the kitchen.

"No!" Timothy screams, reaching for him but missing.

That's when they found them. HE was slumped on the chair by the kitchen table. There was a plate with a half piece of pumpkin pie there, HE had the insides of his body exposed. HE had no head or neck. The head was on the floor with what looked like fingers, part of a heart and tongue in its mouth, still almost trying to chew. Timothy went to shield Earl's eyes from this sight, but he wasn't there. Earl was by the sink kneeling down with his head next to something. It was their mother, Timothy could tell by her apron. It looked like she was trying to say something to Earl. He was placing his ear to her nearly gone face. Timothy quickly pushed Earl to the side taking his place. Timothy wants to hear his mother's last words. Her decimated body was open, exposed internal organs very visible. She had no use of her right arm for it was partially gone, eaten by her. Timothy could barely hear what she was saying. As he got closer he could hear her as plain as day,

"Glory be, glory be." as she chomps on his face.........

# UNPRECEDENTED

Glad to have a day off. The cutbacks at the transit base hurt everyone and I tried not to let it bother me when people left. It really didn't, but Sammy's dismissal bothered me. He'd been a transit driver for a little over a year, he and Char were planning their wedding. They were also finishing up their house for the event when he got called into the depot manager's office. I hated the look on Sammy's face when he left the office. Hell, no time for that now. I'm supposed to be relaxeing and reading my book. I've picked the perfect spot. Well shaded, few bugs, and no people. Granted, I'm a few yards from one of the busiest organic markets in town but I'm near the large stream and it's just me.

"Page one." I sigh, before reading.

Shit, thoughts of Sammy and Char running through my head. Out of the corner of my eye I see a teenage girl by an area of the stream that feeds into the canal. She's taking pictures of something in the water with her cell phone. I wasn't sure what it was. Then she grabs a stick and starts poking it. I bend a little forward to see if I could see what she was really doing and what was in the water that intrigued her so much. As I bend forward more to get a better view, she jumps away from whatever it was, slips and falls in the water. Her actions startled me, causing me to hit the back of my head on the tree. Seconds later I look in her direction and to my surprise she's running frantically towards me. Her mouth is wide open in scream mode with no sound coming out . Her arms are flailing, reaching desperately behind her. Something is on her back. She runs straight towards me then drops a few feet from where I sit. Jumping up to help her, I stop short when I see what's on her back. This thing, this weird looking thing, has encased her entire back, her shoulders down to the top of her waist. There's a horrible stench coming from her. The smell reminds me quickly of the time my brother and I as kids found a dead man on our playground tangled in the monkey bars. I cover my nose with my book, trying to see if the poor girl is moving. She wasn't. But it is. Purplish white, green and black with a shine to it although I think that came from the water. Its pulsating movements were horrid and the damned thing has a tail slowly moving around her butt much like a tadpole. Faintly I hear a cracking sound and what sounds like teeth gnawing. I need to get help. Jumping over the small natural wall by the stream I start yelling for assistance. Many people hear me and look in my direction but only two came to our aid. One was the tall black guy who I'd seen many times before, he worked at the market. The other was a white woman who had just gotten out of her car.

As they run over I look back at the girl while I cover my nose with my book. She, the girl, was no longer there. Stepping closer, now clenching my nose with my fingers, I look all over, nothing, not a trace. Just that God-awful smell. Boldly I go to the spot I knew she was lying. No blood, no bones, no water, nothing but the imprint of what seems like something slid into the water.

"Hey sir, what's wrong!?" The Black guy yells.

Looking in his direction I see he and the woman are overwhelmed by the smell.

"She was right here! She had this thing on her back and it was eating her. Ya'll smell that stench don't you! Look, see, there was something here." I said, pointing to the imprint in the ground.

"Sir, there's nothing here but you and stink." The woman said, turning back towards her car.

"I assure you both I am not crazy, there was a young girl here that was attacked by some kind of animal or something." I said, pleading to the Black guy who I think sort of believed me because I saw he was still looking down at the stream.

"Maybe sir, you should call the police." The Black guy said.

"Police? Yeah, the police." I said, as running by him to get to my car where I left my cell.

Getting to my car, I grab my cell dialing 911 and begin explaining my issue to the operator as I look back at the stream. With my cell phone in tow, I start walking back towards the stream still covering my nose.

"Yes, the market on Ginger st." I tell the operator.

I'm now back at the stream bank but the Black guy isn't around. I look around. I know he did not walk past me, then I see his employee cap on the edge of the stream.

"OH Shit!"

"Excuse me Sir!" was the voice of the operator; I forgot I was still on the line with her.

"Look miss, something is definitely wrong here, another person just vanished, get someone here quick." I said, hanging up.

I stand there staring at his cap briefly when I turn and run to the market. Rushing past shoppers to get to the customer service desk.

"Excuse me, excuse me." I said, impatiently.

"Hi sir, how may I help you?" asks this smiling young lady.

"Hi, I'm looking for an employee of yours, tall Black African guy" I said.

"Is there a problem sir?"

"No, he was helping me with my groceries and we struck up a conversation and I forgot to ask him a question about his country, that's all."

"Do you know his name sir?

"No, but he's very tall, very friendly and speaks French."

"Oh Philippe, just a minute sir, I'll page him".

"Philippe, please come to Customer Service, Philippe please come to Customer Service desk." I hear over the intercom.

I wait patiently for Philippe. Nervously I'm looking around the market looking for him and looking at the faces of the shoppers who have no idea what hell occurred outside a few minutes ago. Five minutes pass, no Philippe. The young lady pages him again when I see her get approached by a coworker. Her smile went away as they were speaking; the smile comes back as she approaches me.

"Sir, I'm afraid Philippe has left the premises for lunch." She tells me.

I nod 'ok' while smiling, when I see through the window behind her emergency lights flashing. I thank her and head towards the door. When I walk outside I see a Police Officer parked by the stream, he gets out of his car and looks towards the stream. I'm walking towards him then he notices me and starts walking towards me. He says something into his shoulder radio. There were a few on-lookers but nothing too big.

"Good afternoon officer." I said.

"Good afternoon sir, may I help you?"

"Oh, I'm sorry; I'm the one that called 911. My name is Eric, Eric Brooks, officer.' I said.

"Officer Norris. So Mr. Brooks can you tell me what happened."

I start explaining to Officer Norris the events. I point to Philippe's cap, still floating in the stream, and the indentation in the mud by the edge of the stream. Officer Norris breaks out his flashlight and proceeds to the indentation and the hat. He notices the faint weird smell in the air, looks at me then continues down the bank.

By now there are about 10 or so people watching from the edge of the parking lot next to the stream.

"You think you wanna call back up!?" I yell to Officer Norris.

He looks at me smiling.

"I'll assess the situation sir, thank you." Officer Norris said.

I frown, stepping away from the stream while stepping up on the parking lot pavement. Officer Norris pulls the hat from the water and places an item next to the hat. He does the same to the indentation and other things; I guess those items he was placing were evidence markers. All the while I'm still hoping Philippe will be somewhere in the crowd of people looking. My attention is jogged when I hear this man coming out of the market yelling, running to us.

"Officer, officer!!!

We all turn in his direction; all except Officer Norris who had crouched down to closely examine something. He wasn't sure what it was and was about to pick it up with his tweezers but thought twice about it. Instead he places a marker next to it. Officer Norris looks up at the yelling man who's now on the parking lot edge with us. It's the young man that was talking to the nice young lady at Customer Service.

"Officer, one of my employees is missing. He was here, helping someone. I think with groceries to their car and now he's gone. His stuff is still here in his locker and he didn't clock out. He's worked here for five years and never once forgotten to clock out for lunch or anytime he leaves! Something ain't right." the young man said.

Officer Norris looks at the young man and starts to walk towards us when suddenly his mouth gapes open with no sounds coming out, just like the girl from earlier. Officer Norris couldn't move. He turns his head to the side to look behind him when he sees that thing has attached itself to his leg. It, that thing, was spreading rapidly up his body. Then that putrid smell returns. Officer Norris somehow manages to get to his gun, firing several shots into it but shoots himself instead. As Officer Norris falls, that ghastly smell and the eating intensifies. The onlookers begin screaming and running back to their cars. Two bold souls try to run to Officer Norris's aid but I grab them, pointing out that it's useless. They see the hell, plus the stench was far too great for any of us to bare. We all hurriedly back away all the while hearing Officer Norris's shoulder radio in the distance,

"Officer Norris, are you still at Pure Foods market? Officer Norris!?"

Then silence.

"What the hell just happened?!!" one of the men I had stopped asks.

All I could do was shrug my shoulders and continue on away from the site. I did manage to say,

"I really have no idea what that thing is or what really just happened but I do know that within the last 45 minutes or so, that thing has killed three people."

"We've got to get help and let the police, the military, hell everyone know what happened here!!" the other gentleman said.

Staring blankly at this guy, I realize there are a lot more witnesses to this and the police do know that Officer Norris responded to this call. I nod at them both and run to Officer Norris's car. I grab the radio microphone and start yelling,

"Officer down, Officer Norris is down!!!" I said.

I was about to repeat what I had just yelled into the police radio when I hear, "This is dispatcher 420, you are not authorized to use this frequency, please refrain...."

"Ma'am, this is Eric Brooks, I made the 911 call from Pure Foods market that Officer Norris responded to. Officer Norris is dead ma'm, repeat Officer Norris is dead. We need help, lots of help here as soon as possible."

"Are you still at the location?" she asks.

"Yes!" I said.

"How many perpetrators are there?" she then asks.

"One, I think."

"Was anyone else hurt? Are you hurt?"

"No, no one, just Officer Norris!" I yell.

"Units are on the way sir. Stay hidden until they arrive sir." dispatcher 420 states.

This is followed by,

"All units 10-00 at Pure Foods market, 1990 Pajma st, this is dispatcher 420, code 10-00 at Pure Foods market, 1990 Pajma st."

I guess I'll sit here patiently for the police. As I wait, those gross images of the two deaths spurt through my head. This is disrupted by a voice.

"Excuse me sir, sir, excuse me."

I look up and there is this light skinned, eyeglasses sporting, fresh faced teen boy with a big ass Mod Squad Linc afro holding a tablet in his hand smirking at me.

"Yes, what kid!?" I yell, pissed off that he's here in this dangerous situation.

His smirk changes to a 'f-u man' look.

"All that shit that went down, I got on video."

"Video?"

"Yeah dude, video, in case you want to show 5-0 when they come."

I perk up as the kid starts the video. Watching it again was even more horrific than I thought. That thing on the back of Officer Norris was the same thing that attacked the girl. Purple, white, green and black with a shine to it and that damned tail. I look away from the video grimacing.

'Stop it kid, please."

"Name's Omar." The kid said, extending his hand.

Reaching out, shaking his hand, we hear tires screeching into the parking lot. Looking up, we see five police vehicles, four unmarked cars and a tactical van. The officers jump out of the vehicles and begin clearing everyone from the parking lot as well as exiting the shoppers from the market via the rear entrance. They set up a perimeter on the outer portion of the parking lot when I see one of the officers snatch his car radio microphone.

'This is Captain Thomas of the Baltimore City Police Tactical Unit, Please come out with your hands up, we have the place surrounded!"

My God, they have no idea what's going on here. I motion for Omar to crouch down low behind Officer Norris's patrol car. I see the loudspeaker switch on the car radio's base and I flick it up and start speaking,

'Captain Thomas, this is Eric Brooks, I made the 911 call Officer Norris responded to. I also called you guys from Officer Norris's car radio for help. There is no one here with guns or any type of weapon here. Officer Norris was attacked by something that came from the water sir."

Silence.

"How do we know you're telling the truth? We know nothing about you!" Captain Thomas yells back.

I sat back to think. I looked around for some sort of answer or something when I saw it. Omar was wearing the whitest button down shirt I'd seen in a while.

"Give me your shirt." I said to Omar.

"What?"

"Your shirt, I need a surrender flag so they won't shoot me." I said, motioning for the shirt. I grab the shirt and wrap it around Officer Norris's baton.

"Captain Thomas, I'm coming out, please do not shoot me!!" I yell through the loudspeaker.

Raising my arms with the baton draped in white, I hesitate, when I hear,

"Hold your fire!" from the other loudspeaker.

Standing up, still nervous, I walk away from the patrol car. I had gotten about 20 feet when five officers rush me to the ground, searching me. All the while I was trying to tell them about Omar but two other officers had already accosted him when I yell to them to be careful with that tablet. Ignoring me, one of the officers speaks into his shoulder radio, giving Captain Thomas the 'all clear'. He's coming our way and I begin telling him of the events that took place here. During my faster than usual talking, I then point towards Omar and the tablet in one of the officers hand.

"Start the video on the tablet. You'll see what I was saying, it's right there." I said.

Captain Thomas starts the video but I couldn't bare to watch it again so I instead watched him and his men watch it. When it ended, Captain Thomas looks at me, then his men.

"This some kinda prank shit or what, captain?" One of his men blurts out.

"It's no prank; I saw this thing kill another person before it got to Officer Norris." I yell at the officers.

Blank looks. Captain Thomas and his men walk to the edge of the parking lot towards the stream.

"This water smells like shit!!"

"It smells worse when that thing comes out!" I yell.

"This thing, on the video, how do we get it to come out?" asks Captain Thomas.

"Why you asking me, I have no clue!" I replied.

"Well Mr. Brooks, right now you're the resident expert on this thing!" Captain Thomas said.

In the background I hear one of the officers yell.

"Isabelle, you and Laboo set up an area upstream. Logan, you Mario and Bville ya'll go downstream."

As Captain Thomas's men hustled about, he himself escorts me and Omar towards the market.

'Look, right now I'd like for you two to stay here at the market, our command post is gonna be set up here. From what I've seen this thing is very dangerous and we've already evacuated the premises, we want you and the young man to be safe."

Omar agreed. I too agree, only because anything that goes on will come through the command post first and I want to know what's going on.

Time drags into nothingness as Omar and myself are put up with two cots and blankets. Within a few hours Omar was fast asleep. I wasn't too far behind but I can't sleep. I'm hungry so I get up to get something to eat. We are, in a market. Walking through the various aisles I see many products with the words "No GMO's" printed on them. I know what 'GMO' stands for, genetically modified organism. Pure Foods prided itself in selling foods that contained no GMO's. I had gotten to the cookie aisle when I see Captain Thomas talking to someone near the opening of a very large tent outside. The person he's talking to didn't seem like a Pure Foods employee or one of his own men. Whoever it was, Captain Thomas was listening and not talking much. Maybe this guy is his superior but in plain clothes. I watch them further as they both look down, it's the tablet they're looking at. The glow off the video gave me a good look at the guy Captain Thomas is with. He looks familiar, but I can't place him. One of Captain Thomas's men comes up to them both.

"Colonel Byrd from the Agency would like to talk to you."

What'd you know, driving the city bus and trying to figure out what people are saying behind me in the mirror by reading their lips firkin works.

When that officer approached them the other gentleman raised his head and it clicked. I know that face. It was Dr. Ito from the Cheyney Univ Applied Physics Lab. Dr. Ito's a genius in his field of Genetic Modifications. Why is he here and what's the deal with this

'Agency' getting involved?

Another question I have is was why'd Captain Thomas lie, saying the command post would be the market when it obviously isn't. To think, all I wanted to do was read my damned book on my damned day off.

On the shelf in front of me I see another thing I've never seen before, organic pop-tarts, pomegranate flavor. I'm hungry so I grab a box. Not going to try to get any sleep now. Working my way to the door that leads to the tent and Dr. Ito. One of Captain Thomas's men sees me and steps in my way. I stop.

"Hi Dr. Ito, I'm a great admirer of your work. Love your book on the Deany Corp genetically modified seeds and what it does to crops and humans!" I yell.

Dr. Ito smiles, thanks me as Captain Thomas rudely interjects,

"Dr. Ito, Mr. Brooks was just saying goodnight. Weren't you Mr. Brooks!?"

Dr. Ito's face distorts with confusion by this outburst.

"Come on Captain, why can't I party with the rest of you? I'm the one that got this thing started."

Captain Thomas seemed like he was about to get a bit physical with me when a resounding voice fills the air.

"He Stays!!"

We all look to see who's just saved me. A giant of a man makes his way from the darkness, way over 6 feet in height, a good muscular 250 lbs or so in black fatigues. This man has a long puffy scar on his left cheek and that 'No Bullshit Taken' look embedded in his face.

"Yes sir Colonel Byrd. Sir" Captain Thomas said, begrudgingly.

Interesting. Local cop, renowned scientist and now some 'Agency' yahoo. Federal dudes trump state dudes.

"Captain, I'd like to see this video. Place it on the big screen." Colonel Byrd said.

The video was loaded. We all watch, again, even me this time.

"Captain Thomas, what are we working with here!?" Colonel Bryd bellows.

"Well sir, I've had the stream cordoned off two miles upstream and five miles downstream. It hasn't moved in five hours sir." Captain Thomas replied.

Weird. Captain Thomas and Colonel Bryd seem to know one another, like they worked together before. Plus those coordinates were strange to me.

"Why two miles up-stream and five miles down-stream were things cordoned off?" I ask.

"That's on a need-to-know basis and you don't need to know." Captain Thomas said.

"Oh really? How do you know it hasn't moved?" I ask, looking at Colonel Bryd for a reaction.

Suddenly, Dr. Ito replays the video, stopping everyone.

"Unprecedented." Dr. Ito repeatedly says, shaking his head.

Omar, who's now awake, comes forward between me and the soldiers.

"What's so damned unprecedented about that thing?" Omar asks.

"We've got movement sir!!" one of Captain Thomas's men yells out.

We all rush to the radar screen albeit Omar and I have a soldier escort. It surprises me that they let us stay for this. On the large radar screen we see a large red circle moving upward. Captain Thomas indicates that it's moving upstream. That notice was, I'm sure, not directed to me and Omar.

"Isabelle, Laboo, get ready!" Captain Thomas barks in his walkie-talkie.

The blip is still moving upward on the screen.

"Hold steady, it's coming pretty fast."

"We still don't have a visual yet sir." was the response.

We're all still looking at the screen when suddenly the blip just stops. A few seconds pass, nothing. Colonel Byrd snatches the walkie-talkie from Captain Thomas.

"Agents!! What's your status! Now!!" Colonel Byrd yells into the walkie-talkie.

Complete silence then Colonel Byrd yells again into the walkie-talkie.

"Agents!!!"

We then hear the crackle of a transmission trying to come through.

"Sorry sir, we thought we had a visual, but nothing sir." the voice said.

All are still staring at the radar screen as I began wondering what happened and why did Colonel Byrd call those officers "Agents". In a flash the blip starts moving again. This time downward on the screen. Towards where we are. I see Dr. Ito writing vigorously in his notepad, walking outside the tent, perhaps back to the market or to the stream to see this thing. No one but me seems to notice him and like a dummy, I follow him outside. He continues to write in his notepad as it's confirmed that he's walking to the stream. Does he not remember what that thing did in the video? I slow down and watch from a distance. Sudden gushes of air fly past me; it's the police/agents running with rifles and guns towards where Dr. Ito is now standing. I stayed where I was for several good reasons, I thought. Three of Captain Thomas's men had switched on these huge spotlights that they had setup during the night. They guide their beams towards the stream. Everything was quiet and still when one of the spotlights catches large bubbles piercing the water's surface in one part of the stream. Fiercely and violently the water's surface explodes skyward cascading down upon this large immense entity. It's eight to ten feet in height, maybe five to seven feet in width. The size is amazing but its shape was more astounding and very grotesque in every sense. It sort of looks like the thing that was on that poor girl's back. The spotlight reflects off of its shiny translucent purplish green skin. It now has arms. Six of them, all different sizes. Looking closer, I see, My GOD, those are the arms of the people it's attacked. They're actually moving to shield its many eyes which too are from the people and things it's attacked, from the bright light. My fascination becomes a squeamish terror as I see parts of that young girl, Officer Norris and Phillipe intertwined with its own body. Still with the malformed nature of that thing's body its dimensions looked quite familiar. That thing is three quarters of the way out of the water when gunfire erupts. As each bullet strikes the creature a horrible wailing sound is heard coming from it. The creature stops, moves onto the shore then stops. The gunfire was nonstop which only seems to make it mad. Several more rounds are emptied into the beast as it quickly turns its unnatural form to submerge back into the water, still wailing away. Captain Thomas and his men run to the shore, continuing their firing into the water to where the creature used to be. In all that was happening I had forgotten about Dr. Ito. Scanning in the direction to where he was I don't see him. Getting more frightened my mind triggers morbid thoughts. I didn't think the creature got close enough to get Dr. Ito so where is he? Oh no! I thought to myself, I hope he didn't get shot. I was already running to the last place I saw him. Frantically searching, I finally spot him. He's on the ground, face down, not moving. Shit, he was shot.

"Dr. Ito! Dr. Ito!" I scream.

Hurridley I knelt down to check on him. As my hand reaches his shoulder he slowly turns his head.

"Yes?!" Dr. Ito exclaims.

Stopping for a second, I begin giving him the physical once over, checking for bullet holes.

"Are you ok? Did you get hit?"

"No, I'm fine.'

"What happened to the organism?" Dr.Ito asks, as I'm still checking for bullet holes when he brushes my hands off of him.

"Fine! The posse shot it many times, it stopped, made a weird noise then went back into the water."

Dr. Ito looks back at the stream.

"They didn't kill it."

"How do you know?" I asked.

Dr. Ito ignores while he's reaching to the ground to pick up his notebook. That's when we see Colonel Byrd, Captain Thomas and his men walking towards us with victory all over their faces.

"You two ok?" Colonel Byrd asked.

We both shake our heads 'yes'. Colonel Byrd instantly turns to Captain Thomas.

"Wrap it up here Captain."

Dr. Ito and I gaze at them all in amazement. When Dr. Ito steps forth.

"It's not dead Colonel."

Everyone got quiet. Colonel Byrd smirks.

"Dr. Ito I'm sure all that firepower was more than enough to kill that thing."

Dr. Ito smirks back, repeating what he said earlier.

"It's not dead. You only made it mad, you may have injured it and it probably went to regenerate or heal itself."

Colonel Byrd is seething.

"What makes you so damned sure of that Dr. Ito!?!"

Dr. Ito, sensing the hostility, backs away from Colonel Byrd.

"I don't know." Dr. Ito said, mildly.

This time a frown erupts on Colonel Byrd's face, the kind that squoze his eyebrows together adjusting the placement of his hat on his head.

'You don't know!? Did you just say 'you don't know?' Well dammit I do." Colonel Byrd snarls.

In that confrontation, Colonel Byrd turns to one of his men.

"Shine a light on the water, let's see if there is any residual damage."

The officer/agent rushed to the spotlight. For some crazy reason I found this moment to yell out.

"You assholes are NSA aren't you!!!?"

They all turn in my direction without any expression.

"We're all friends now, so stop lying!!" I yell.

Colonel Byrd quickly steps to me as Dr. Ito hastily moves away from me. He's about three inches from my face with the odor of fading cheap cologne and pungent mustard.

"Can you give Doc and your little friends a ride home? It'll be in their best interest to say 'yes'."

I glance over at Dr. Ito, then to the stream then back to Colonel Byrd who has not moved away from my face. Dr. Ito ushers me away from the Colonel. Omar was standing behind Dr. Ito and me the whole time not saying a word.

"We'd better roll dude!" Omar blurts out.

A fast scour at Omar, then back to Colonel Byrd, I shake my head in disgust. Reluctantly, the three of us head towards my car. Many things are still simmering in my head.

"You both saw that thing, right?"

Both men agree.

"Its shape looked strange but familiar at the same time. I've seen that shape somewhere before but my mind is not registering what it is."

"DNA Helix." Dr. Ito said.

"What?" I said.

"That organism, it's shape, it's a DNA Helix. It seems it's made itself out of all the DNA structures of plants, animals, insects and humans it's consumed. I think those bullets just stunned it, not killed it." Dr. Ito said.

"You've got to be kidding me. That thing is a big glob of DNA of all kinds of shit just mushed together and it's hungry and angry. This is some sci-fi bull doc. I saw that thing and I think it's some government made mistake that's why the colonel and his boys are all here."

"Cool." Omar, chimes.

We are still walking to my car with our escort with me trying to convince the doctor that he's crazy and wrong. Dr. Ito goes on to tell me about an incident in South America and how that DNA Helix organism was caused by Deany Corps use of GMO'S. He continues saying that in that incident, there were no human casualties only livestock, some reptiles and birds. The organism was shot and that killed it, very unlike the one we've encountered..

"What, you've seen this kind of shit before?! What is wrong with you government assholes!?" I yell at Dr. Ito.

His head is sunk down onto his shoulders, turning away from me and Omar.

"Wait a minute. What was all that you were writing in your little book Dr. Ito?" I ask, forcing him to turn to me as I cut off his path.

"I was working on a hypothesis regarding the notion that genetically modified organisms can alter an organic organism to mutant dangerous proportions. The agency knows of my work and Deany Corps practices are on their radar screen. None, except those who needed to know, are aware of the incident in South America." Dr. Ito said.

I look briefly at Omar's young face, vacant of any emotion.

"So the government knew and we are guinea pigs to see what would happen!" I scream, getting closer to Dr. Ito.

Omar quickly cuts between the two of us. With our escorts encouraging us to keep moving.

"Yes and no. Yes the government knew about South America but, no, we had no idea about the grandeur of what was going on here."

"This shit is just crazy, pure D crazy!" Omar yells out, motioning feverishly with his hands between Dr. Ito and myself.

"This is what happens when man plays GOD and Satan at the same time." Dr. Ito said.

We were stuck in the confusion and anger of what was being said. None of us noticed that Colonel Byrd, his men along with our escort were hustling toward the stream.

"Oh shit, oh shit, it's got Isabelle!!" followed by heavy gunfire.

The three of us duck behind my car. From my vantage point I see the stream, the agents and the organism. It was back. The bullets are not having the same effect it had earlier.

"Dr. Ito, the bullets aren't stunning it like before, why!?" I yell.

Dr. Ito glances up, staring at the organism. His facial expression rapidly changes.

"My GOD. The organism consumed that man with the Kevlar vest, now its DNA has messed with the armor in the vest now its bullet proof." Dr. Ito exclaims.

Amidst the gunfire and the organism's slow approach towards Colonel Byrd and his men, Dr. Ito knew he had to get Colonel Byrd's attention somehow. That soon became easy to do as the colonel, Captain Thomas and their men make a hasty retreat into the market with me, Dr. Ito and Omar right behind them. Once in the market Dr. Ito grabs Colonel Byrd.

"The organism cannot be killed with bullets now, its body has taken the guise of the Kevlar vest, there has to be another way." Dr.Ito said, "Captain, where are your explosives?"

"We've got several grenades on hand; the rocket launcher and rockets are in the tent outside sir."

Without hesitation, Captain Thomas points to two of his men.

"Laboo, Bville, see if you can introduce the organism to some grenades!"

Without saying a word, the two agents head to the front of the market. I watch them as they slowly move from one aisle to another. I myself knew it wasn't in the market yet, there isn't that foul smell. Climbing to the top of the shelf of the aisle I am in, I look in the direction of the front window where the customer service desk is located. There I see the organism outside the window in the parking lot. It's moving around but very slowly.

Laboo and Bville find it too. They both began launching grenades through the window onto the organism. Two large explosions are followed by two more, where after each, the organism appears to shiver then emits a loud grunting bestial sound. Those explosions crumble the market's wall, enabling the beast's horrid smell to blanket the inside of the market. Agent Laboo rises up to fire another grenade but he's greeted with what has the features of tentacles encircling his body. His screaming out in agony echoes off the vaulted ceiling of the market as his writhing body tries desperately to free itself.

Agent Bville rushes to the organism with knife in hand to cut agent Laboo free but he too becomes entangled in the man-made hell. Their insides are splattered along the aisles and the walls of the market. By this time, all are seeing what I'm seeing.

"The vines act as tentacles. From the plants it's consumed. Remarkable." Dr. Ito said, astonished.

"So those weren't tentacles?" I asked.

Once again Colonel Byrd, Captain Thomas and the remaining agents, open fire. In close quarters the gunfire was deafening. I cover my ears while watching the organism move closer and closer to them. Suddenly a few aisles away from the organism I see one of the agents. He's walking directly up on it. In his left hand I see he has a medium size kerosene tank. "What is he trying to do?" I think to myself. Then the agent opens the top of the kerosene tank, throwing it at the organism. Kerosene splatters all over it. The agent pulls the pin on a grenade and he throws that too onto the organism. A large boom is immediately followed by a huge ball of fire. Within the flames we could see it stopped moving. Then the sprinklers go off.

"Shit, Shit Shit!!" the agent screams out.

Now the organism starts moving again, away from the agents' location, but towards me, Dr.Ito and Omar.

"Hey, ya'll high tail it out of there now!" Colonel Byrd shouts at us.

He didn't have to tell Omar twice, for he saw an opportunity earlier when the organism was motionless, he bolted out the front door. Our exit was now blocked by the organism and it extends more vines looking for anything to consume. Dr. Ito and I were headed away from the organism when we see another agent a few yards in front of the organism. He had what looks like a time bomb on his chest.

"Dr. Ito!! Hey Dr. Ito!!" The agent shouts out.

"Yes Agent?" Dr. Ito replies.

"That thing, it becomes whatever it eats right!?" the agent asks.

"Something like that, agent" Dr. Ito yells.

"Well doc, I've got this homemade, well, market made, bomb on my person, set for 2 min, if I have that thing eat me with this on then I can kill it right? Blow it up from the inside?" the agent yells out.

"Strong possibility agent but not sure."

Just then, we all hear a loud booming voice.

"Agent Mario, you are out of line. Resume your position and defuse that device, that's a direct order!" Captain Thomas bellows.

"Sorry Captain, some drastic shit needs to be done now!!" agent Mario yells, as he starts walking fast towards the organism.

"Archibald Mario is my name, you ungodly mother....!!" The agent screams as he hurls himself into the organism.

"NO!!!" Captain Thomas screams.

The organism now has agent Mario inside of it, and we all see he is still able to move around inside the organism, but with jerky puppet-like movements. Two minutes are up. In slow motion, Archibald Mario's body separates into pieces; blood, arms, legs, head and torso expand throughout the organism. Once again, the organism begins moving slowly. It moves to the right then suddenly it collapses onto its side, motionless. The stench coming from it now has gotten greater as we witness its insides smoldering. Dr. Ito and I are observing it from a good distance but we are close enough to see clearly that maybe it's dead. Colonel Byrd and the others weren't so sure. They all slowly meander towards the laid out creature. As they get closer, one of the agents fires his weapon several times into the organism causing everyone to stop, staring at the shooter.

"What?" He says.

They then continue on.

"Is it dead sir?" One of the agents asks, looking at Captain Thomas for reassurance.

"I don't really know agent."

"Dr. Ito, we may need your expertise and diagnosis!" Colonel Byrd shouts.

"I can help you from here!" Dr. Ito yells back.

I'm laughing when I notice in one of the mirrors on the ceiling that Colonel Byrd has picked up a long silver thin rod from the ground. It's the rod used by market staff to reach items on the top shelf. He begins poking the organism when I jump up screaming.

"No! Don't do that!!"

My outburst surprises everyone, but the following seconds horrifies them. The organisms' vine-like tentacles and the human arms of the ones consumed, grapple Colonel Byrd, Captain Thomas and the remaining agents. Gunfire, screams and cursing reverberate harshly from the bloody market ceiling and walls. I can't stomach watching the carnage. Taking a grip of Dr. Ito, I bolt to the rear of the market. Luckily, we find a door unlocked that leads to the market's storage area. Scanning the area quickly, I'm looking for a rear exit to this room but there is none. No windows either, just the air vent shaft in the ceiling. Dr. Ito, his face tired and worn, continues writing in his book.

"Dr. Ito, What are you writing now?" I asked.

He ignores me and keeps on writing.

"Dr. Ito….."

"If you must know I'm writing my last will and testament." Dr. Ito, exasperates.

My face squelches up as I walk away to listen to what's going on outside. Placing my ear against the door I hear nothing, total silence. Just as I was pulling away from the door, I hear items falling off the shelves hitting the floor. Listening more intently, I hear the noise again but this time it seems closer than before.

"It's coming."

Dr. Ito looks up from his notepad, now I can see fright blossom from his eyes. I motion for him to get some stuff to prop against the door. He points to a large desk not far from the door. Without haste we place it against the door followed by a big swivel chair, several large boxes and a floor waxeer.

"Trying to give it indigestion I see." whispers a smiling Dr. Ito.

"If this stuff kills it I'll give all the money I have to buy the company's stock."

That bit of humor is short-lived as the door rattles. We quickly race away from the door and hide behind several large boxes. While we were hunkering down, I notice Dr. Ito staring at a very large box on the second shelf where we're hiding. Reaching up, he tries to obtain it but it's too heavy for him and it comes crashing to the ground with a loud thud. Looking at each other silently; each hoping that thing didn't or couldn't hear the box falling. Instinctively, we jump up pushing the box against the door as quietly as we can. In doing so, I slip on some leakage from the box and almost fell but regain my balance. The door rattles again. We both dive, well actually slide, back into our hiding spot. Slowly, the door starts to open and our barrage is easily moved out of the way. It's now fully in the room and it's gotten larger. Remnants of Colonel Byrd, Captain Thomas and the others are grossly visible inside and outside of the organism. Dr. Ito and I sit there quietly, awaiting our death, waiting for one of the vines to corral us or something. In our wait, I notice that the boxes we're behind are boxes from the Deany Corporation, it's Weed Killer. This is the stuff that's genetically modified to kill the bugs but not the plant. I see the organism in the reflection of the stuff that spilled onto the floor. That too is from a Deany Corp box. The organism stops. It seems as though it's backing away from the stuff on the floor. On the floor to my left is a bag of chocolate chip cookies that had fallen off the shelf too. I have an idea.

Getting Dr. Ito's attention, I pick up the bag and toss it into the liquid on the floor in front of the organism. Splash from that liquid gets on the creature and sends it into a frenzy. Another idea flashes; I tear open a Deany Corp box. Inside are four 24 oz. containers full of Weed Killer with the spray gun attached. I leap up spraying the hell out of the organism. The first few sprays hit it dead on. The organism shakes then makes a quick move towards me. I retreat, never stopping my spraying. It was about maybe 10 feet away when I see Dr. Ito spraying too. That slows it down. Suddenly, the terrible smell it's emitting has changed. It's more putrid and now has the smell of ammonia. It's backing away from us fast, going back to the door. Making its way out of the room, it tears itself to the front of the market. We snatch several bottles of the weed killer and head after it. It's moving pretty fast for a creature with so much girth, amazing. The intense ammonia smell doesn't waver. It has us gasping for air as tears dwindle down our cheeks. We, however, never stop spraying.

The organism makes it out of the hole in the wall by customer service caused by the earlier grenades.

"It's headed for the stream!" Dr. Ito yells.

Frantically rushing to it, the two of us are in the parking lot near Officer Norris's patrol car. Dr. Ito is on his third container of spray. I'm on my fourth. Our continued spraying definitely slows it down. It has trouble navigating the natural wall on the edge of the parking lot near the stream. Now we're spraying emptiness from the containers. Still, it's moving away from us, managing to get to the bank of the stream. Abruptly its movement ceases and its size begins diminishing, going back to its original size when it was enveloped on that poor girl's back. Vestiges of what wasn't fully consumed lay strewn across the bank; arms, legs, heads, uniforms, guns.

"I don't think we should let it get in the water!" Dr. Ito exclaims.

"What the hell do you want me to do about that!?" I shout.

Promptly, Dr. Ito picks up a large stick from the ground and pours the remaining weed killer onto it. Exhaling deeply he glances at me. I instantly knew what he wanted me to do. Without hesitation, I take the stick from him, leap over the natural wall, landing me a few feet from the organism. It's maybe two or three feet from the water itself, still moving, but very slow and weak. Smaller now, but nonetheless menacing.

"Don't wait dammitt!!" Dr. Ito yells.

Glancing quickly in his direction, I regain my thoughts as to why I'm here. I raise the stick driving it hard into the organism. It shudders, makes a weird non distinct noise floundering on the bank like a hooked fish. The force of my drive impales it into the stream's bank, stopping its movement. With its last moments, it absorbs an item, hopefully for the last time. The stick covered with the Deany Corporation weed killer. Unprecedented, the genetically modified residue that gave it life ultimately destroys it.

THE END

# *ACKNOWLEDGMENTS*

Cover Art Photo, Donna Spencer
Manuscript Format, Chrita Paulin, Coal Under Pressure Publications
Author Photo, Andrew George
The Middleton Family
The Norris Family
The Baltimore City College HS Family
The Cheyney University of PA Family
Frostburg State University Family
Dr. Eugenia Collier

**Joseph Norris, III**

Joseph Norris III, native of Baltimore, MD, was raised in Cherry Hill in Southern Baltimore city. Joseph attended the prestigious Baltimore City College High School. After High School, Joseph attended the Alpha of All HBCU's in America, Cheyney State College, as it was called in 1982. Currently, it's named Cheyney University of PA. In 1984 Joseph transferred to Frostburg State University in the mountains of Western Maryland due to financial hardships. Before graduating from Frostburg's mountainous remote campus, Joseph would tell his suitemates and others, scary tales about the monsters in the woods surrounding the school.

In 1990 Joseph was involved in a near fatal car accident. While he was in the hospital, Joseph would tell his family, friends and nurses many crazy, weird, strange stories that he made up while lying in the hospital bed for those long 6 months. After a year and a half of outpatient rehab Joseph then went back to school. That summer, Joseph took a Creative Writing Course at Morgan State Univ. He signed up for that class and wowed his professor with the reading of his first story. Of course, it was a story that was macabre and scary. With training from the course professor, Dr. Eugenia Collier, his stories got better, more weird and terrifying. Joseph had found his niche. Well, years went past, jobs came and went, Joseph would still dabble with writing but he thought of it as a joyous hobby until he started writing a story he had thought of while in the hospital, that story developed into "The Shepherd Into Hell" book.

Joseph is ready to scare the hell out of you. "It gives me great joy when a person reads one of my stories and they tell me that they have altered their route, their way of doing things, don't go anywhere alone now and they always ask "what where you thinking!?" I love it. "Thanks all, and remember, always be afraid of that creak you hear in the night."

CPSIA information can be obtained
at www.ICGtesting.com
Printed in the USA
BVHW042138020622
638802BV00004B/43